5-23-17

ST. JOAN'S ARCHITECT

Rohn of Federbush

LifeRich Publishing is a registered trademark of The Reader's Digest Association, Inc.

LifeRich Publishing books may be ordered through booksellers or by contacting:

LifeRich Publishing
1663 Liberty Drive
Bloomington, IN 47403
www.liferichpublishing.com
1 (888) 238-8637

Because of the dynamic nature of the Internet, any web addresses or links contained in this book may have changed since publication and may no longer be valid. The views expressed in this work are solely those of the author and do not necessarily reflect the views of the publisher, and the publisher hereby disclaims any responsibility for them.

Any people depicted in stock imagery provided by Thinkstock are models, and such images are being used for illustrative purposes only.
Certain stock imagery © Thinkstock.

ISBN: 978-1-4897-0775-8 (sc)
ISBN: 978-1-4897-0776-5 (e)

Print information available on the last page.

LifeRich Publishing rev. date: 6/2/2016

St. Joan's Architect

A fledgling architect, Catherine Marksteiner's graduation trip to Mont Saint Michel includes a visit from St. Joan's ghost, who takes advantage of Catherine's abilities. History says the saint went missing for four months. Was Mont Saint Michel her destination and the site of Joan's betrayal into the hands of the English? Now St. Joan wants a glass dome addition for the unused platform in front of St. Michael's to house butterflies in her honor. Catherine is not sure who is rendering the intricate drawings in her sketch pad but she's fallen in love with the island and wants to marry a citizen. She isn't told the artist who sketches her is already engaged, but his smitten cousin Romèe is ready to offer his father's shipping fortune and Vatican connections as well as his hand in marriage.

Finalist: Heart of the West, RWA Utah, 2001

By

Rohn of Federbush

2016

2141 Pauline Court, Ann Arbor MI 48103
www.rohnfederbush.com
rohn@comcast.net, 734-994-6217

PROLOGUE

June, Ann Arbor, Michigan

"I'm kissing all the rooms good-bye," Catherine Marksteiner's mother said. "Are you ready? In fifteen minutes the cab arrives. Then we're off to chase St. Joan's ghost around Mont Saint Michel."

Catherine nodded. Their life in Ann Arbor would end after this trip. Catherine would join students in Lansing's School of Architecture and Mother would move to Chicago with her new husband.

Wrongly interpreting Catherine's mood, Mother said, "I'll make sure the movers arrange your room in Chicago exactly as it is now."

"It doesn't matter." Catherine sighed. "I won't see the furniture until Thanksgiving."

"I envy you." Mother sat down on the bare mattress next to Catherine's carry-on bag. "Your grandmother knew I could never survive college."

Catherine shoved her blue nightgown into the nylon bag. "What makes you think I can?" Traces of a disturbing dream floated away before she could recount them.

"No worries. At your age, I hardly spoke to people. And my brain has never entertained a logical thought."

Catherine closed the zipper on her bag. Mother was too wound up with wedding arrangements to consider how unsettling it was *not* to return to the only home Catherine had known for eighteen years.

"I don't see your sketch pads," Mother said

"I packed them away with my school things."

"Won't you need them on Mont Saint Michel?"

Catherine slung her camera bag over her shoulder, careful to keep her long hair from getting snagged. "My digital will do. I don't want tourists crowding me."

"Suit yourself." Mother said. "We're going to have a great trip. Aren't you excited to finally visit the Mont?"

Catherine followed her mother down the circular staircase. "I'm just…." The house echoed their retreating footsteps. "Nothing will ever be familiar again."

At the foot of the staircase, Mother embraced her roughly. "Me. You remember me, don't you?"

Catherine giggled. "Yeah, you I know." Then embarrassed by an unstoppable sob, she blurted, "But you'll be in Chicago with Danny."

Mother hadn't let go, and Catherine didn't struggle. Mother's warmth, her old-fashioned rose perfume, comforted. After all, college was before her. The mysterious future stretched her very bones.

When the cab arrived, a slight breeze dislodged blooms from the magnolia tree. A shower of pink petals littered the yellow taxi. Catherine opened the car's door for her mother. "You just want to be haunted."

"St. Joan might have visited the Mont." Mother argued, "I want to ask her why she keeps haunting writers. Montaigne, Mark Twain and Bernard Shaw were all enchanted with her."

Catherine slid into the back seat next to her mother. "You'll probably end up being visited by a mold-smelling, toady spirit monk and your next paranormal novel will be a best seller."

On the way to the airport Catherine's thoughts turned to the dream of the night before. "I wanted to tell you my dream, but I don't even remember why."

"Joan of Arc." Mother gripped Catherine's arm, as if she recalled the saint's admonishment the same moment Catherine did.

In surprised unison they repeated Joan of Arc's dictate that they had shared, "Why sleepest thou whilst heavens quake? Prepare to tear the cosmic screen serene. If you are the salt of the earth, I am the volcanic mist, the unchangeable syllable."

Mont Saint Michel, 1430

After the siege of Paris, when her Voices abandoned her, the Maid of Orleans went missing from historical records for four months before she was captured. She might have used the time to secure the defenses of Mont Saint Michel with captured English mortars. Her army would have traveled undetected at night, as they did for eleven nights during the trip from Vaucoulers to the uncrowned dauphin in Chinon. The trip from Paris to Mont Saint Michel was even shorter.

The English guarded the entranceway and sold passes to devout pilgrims. Their soldiers lined the shore, out of arrow range, sporting with the shepherdless sheep who would grace their campfires as roasted mutton soon enough. There was plenty of time to starve the French out of their last unconquered home in Normandy. However, the French never lost Mont Saint Michel to the English. In 1430, one-hundred and nineteen knights and their entourages held off the round-headed Englishmen from overtaking the Mont.

And one night in early January against the dark silhouette of the Mont, Joan of Arc might have crept into a dark Avranches stable, escorted only by her confessor. The northern most Normandy coastal town ends where at low tide a surf-free causeway leads to the Mont.

The farmer would have heard the family's cow protest and hurry out to investigate. He found Joan on her knees rapt in prayer. The soldier clothes on the young girl made it clear the Maid of Orleans was praying for all the stolid peasants and rough soldiers of the French nationalists, the Armagnacs. Afraid to startle this marvelous child attuned to the slightest whispering of God, the farmer heeded her monk's plea for silence and slipped out of the barn. He sent his wife with clothes to disguise their new milkmaid.

Brother Richard explained Joan was determined to buy a pass from the English to seek out further instructions from Saint Michael. She'd planned to come on Saint Michael's Day, October 16th, but the Battle of Hastings kept her occupied. She told their French-speaking, Normandy hosts of her comrades falling on the fields of battle for France and worse: losing their faith in her mission at the siege of Paris.

She spoke long into the night about the exploits of her brothers, Jean and Pierre; and her cousins, Durand Laxart and Burey-le-Petit. As well-loved as her family; her early escorts to Chinon from Voucouluers, Jean de Metz and Bertrand de Poulegny, were as loyal and sure hearted as herself. Nevertheless, even the later heroes of her campaigns, General La Hire and the beautiful Dunois, were dead now. All gone.

When Joan's Voices first called her, wolves had roamed the streets of Paris and few provinces south of the Loire held for France. Now, even the King told her how difficult it was to believe unless miracles happen to you.

The day after her first communion in the summer of her thirteenth year, St. Joan heard her Voices while the noon Angelus bells were ringing. She beheld these Visions in her father's garden two paces from the church. In her later trial, she would describe their arrival: "They came as painted in the churches."

Brother Richard noticed the peasant couple's growing disbelief. He chided them, "What can you believe? Cannot God pay attention to a single soul who believes the supernatural world makes itself manifest?"

Joan had grown accustomed to proselytizing critics. "They told me to 'go to France,' two or three times a week. Saint Michael promised the virgin martyrs, Saint Catherine and Saint Margaret, would provide counsel for God's mission to crown the dauphin." Joan offered the monk's cup to their host for a refill of wine. "My Voices spoke of 'the pity that was the kingdom of France'."

The couple could only nod in agreement with that heavenly assessment.

The monk took advantage of their receptiveness. "For four years Joan kept her inspiration secret. Neither I nor her parents knew. But when her father dreamt of Joan on horseback, he threatened to drown her with his own hands so Joan revealed her mission."

Joan shook her cropped head at her father's folly. "In 1428 my Voices became more insistent. They told me, 'If Orleans falls, France is gone. And again, Daughter of God, go forth. I will be your guide'."

The farmer, his wife and Brother Richard watched the future saint look around their kitchen, perhaps expecting to see or hear from her Saints.

Joan hoped if she could get inside Mont Saint Michel, Scotland might offer her refuge. Scottish supplies still ran the blockade behind the Mont, past the bored and sleepy English on Tomberlaine. Moreover, St. Joan trusted Hamish Power, a Scot diplomat. Eleven months before he had presented her with her heraldic standard, fleur-de-lis on white linen with silken gold fringe. She carried it from Orleans to the crowning of King Charles in the Rheims Cathedral. On July 17, 1429, at the Rheims Cathedral, wearing a gold and velvet cloak over her white armor, she held the Scottish-made banner proudly. At the Bishop's objection, Joan of Arc answered, "The banner has borne the burden and it has earned the honor."

Joan told the couple that after Rheims her capricious Voices told her she would, "last but a year."

She sought Saint Michael's enlightenment at Mont Saint Michel and hoped to persuade the helpful Scots into diverting some of their resources to her troops without going through the King's hands.

"She's no sorceress," the farmer's good wife said. "Those horrid Englishmen will sell a pilgrim's pass to a monk fast enough, but a young girl might give them other ideas."

"That new horse blanket," the farmer agreed, "is coarse enough to pass for monk garb."

So it was that Joan of Arc, with her armor well hidden under the religious disguise, set foot inside the gates of Mont Saint Michel. The Scottish envoy was immediately called home for further instructions.

St. Joan wandered, a lost soul seeking God's own ear, among the pilgrims sheltered in the Almonry for three months. Each entablature and capital of the columns held a unique design, varying and vying with its neighbor as did the roscaces and carved foliage on the Cloister pillars; but no spiritual news from St. Michael drifted among their heights.

Hammish Power did return in March of the ill-fated year (1430) and promised Scotland could offer Joan refuge with assurances of ransom if she were captured. The diplomat presented Joan with a great, fur-collared cape; but he had no funds or pledges of continued help for France, no funds for her weary troops famishing in the fields around Paris.

Joan dined with him and several of the off-duty knights in the great hall. The salty mutton stew cheered her into retelling her plans for pushing the English out. She stood at the broad dining table pointing out the advantageous moves her troops could still make. Maps were rolled out, held down with empty bowls of the stew. Sir Cabay, or was it Sir Icabus, asked about the advantage of spring floods again, when Joan first heard the jangle of Saint Catherine's golden bracelets.

Joan looked up to see a young girl's long red hair circling a blue cotton dress high above her. Saint Catherine seemed surprised to see Joan in the dark hall. Moreover, Joan could not remember Saint Catherine's simple frock. Usually she wore layers upon layers of rich embroidered silk. Perhaps this was a sleeping dress.

The present-day Catherine Marksteiner rubbed her eyes as if to confirm she had been sleeping.

The knights were confused by her trance, but Joan's black-robed confessor pulled them back to the fireplace for more stew, explaining their leader's sources of inspiration.

Joan usually felt ecstasy in the presence of her Voices but she realized the awful truth. There would be no plans for her troops to carry out. It was over and the English would not be thrown out. She nestled down into her cape letting the collar cover her ears. Saint Catherine did not seem to have a message. Maybe she would answer a question.

"Shall I be with you soon?" Joan of Arc asked. Catherine, the dreamer answered yes. If dreams hold parts of reality, then St. Joan will always live in the dreams of young girls. But Joan thought Catherine was of her earlier world of saintly Voices and heard the answer as her death sentence.

And in late April when the tide was as high as the highest step at the main gate, supply barges hid along the outer coast of the bay. In the dark of the moon, the only lights to be seen were the campfires of the English on the inland-side of the cove. Faithful lantern holders along the southern side of the island prepared the signal. The empty supply barge left Mont Saint Michel. St. Joan was not surprised when the oarsmen spoke English, or when they tied her arms behind her back. She succumbed long before the fire licked her holy heels.

Mont Saint Michel, June

Five-hundred and seventy-six years later, when the dreamer, Catherine Marksteiner, stepped upon the sacred ground of Mont Saint Michel, St. Joan's spirit welcomed her.

With history threatening to forget her, St. Joan determined France should build an edifice worthy of God's glory on the unconquered rock of Mont Saint Michel, one that St. Joan's enthusiasts could see with their own bodily eyes. She planned the Dome of St. Joan would rise on the empty west platform of the Abbey, a pink crystal greenhouse where butterflies would surround a marble baptismal font. St. Joan determined not to abandon the misty halls leading from earth to heaven until her monument was in place. Every humble woman needed to know their futures were achievable, if they possessed faith in their God-given dreams.

CHAPTER ONE

Mont Saint Michel, June, Saturday

At the southern parapet, Romèe Laurent stood like a captain of a great lumbering ship. The weather held at fifty degrees and white fluffy clouds sprinkled the sparkling sky. The bay's fragrant marsh grasses moved with the wind, while Romèe waited at his post.

Mont Saint Michel's soaring spires, the pink-bleached stones of the outer walls, the sudden splashes of tender gardens within its confines, even the moldy corners on the ancient stairs claimed Romèe's increasing allegiance. No metal detectors, drug-sniffing dogs or arrogant guards were needed to keep out the terrors of the televised world. Tourists felt safe.

"Sirrah, your marriage candidates have arrived." Anton Bermont slapped his cousin's back.

Romèe's dark brows lowered, as he focused on the tour bus below. The morning sun had already warmed the wide stonework under his elbows. Romèe checked his watch: ten o'clock.

The first tour bus in a line of eight pulled as close as possible to the south entrance. Anticipating tips, the bus driver dismounted, then helped each traveler off. A mother and daughter of identical height were his last two passengers. The girl was a beanpole with red hair long enough to sit on.

The ancient pavement under Romèe's feet suddenly lifted.

The slim urchin, who claimed his attention, touched her thick-soled gym shoes to the roots of Mont Saint Michel, or his. The entire island seemed to reach for the heavens. Life itself seemed lighter. Romèe let out a long sigh. His first since spying the redhead.

The girl's white haired mother was plumper, 'zaftig' his father would say, meaning soft and still juicy. Romèe wondered if all sons hated how the words of their parents stuck in their heads.

"Oh, look," Anton teased. "I have another red-headed, Botticelli model."

"This model has her mother as chaperon. You better mind your manners."

His blond older cousin, an artist, deftly managed the eight-unit Hotel de Bermont, which allowed him ample opportunity to sketch. Anton sketched all his hotel guests. Romèe wasn't at all sure his cousin should spend time with the young woman below; until he, Romèe, found the opportunity to talk to her, to see if a brain lay under those long folds of red hair, to see if a spark of interest might be shared between them. Actually, just to see her.

"From the amount of luggage, I'd say they're probably the guests we have booked for the week," Anton said. "The marsh grass spoils even the off-season."

Romèe did not mind the smell of the fresh greenery on
thought the diminished tourist traffic a blessing. "Could you
paint?"

"Your father would kill me." Anton laughed. "You're lucky he hasn't
insisted you become a priest."

"No vocation for the priesthood." Romèe kept his eye on the redhead
below. She chose one of the heavier pink bags from her mother. Affectionate
acts renewed his faith in people. Not everyone was out to better themselves
at someone else's expense. And this daughter, obviously, had been taught
consideration for others.

"But your name means you're destined to visit Rome," Anton taunted.

"'Visit' is the operative word." Romèe smiled. "At least I convinced
my father I had too many women chasing me to seriously consider the
priesthood."

"So it's marriage, is it?"

"Someday," Romèe said. "But, you'll beat me to the altar."

At thirty-two Anton had been engaged for four years to a dark-headed
girl Romèe had only seen once. Providing the orphan a home for a year, Aunt
Gail spirited her off to a mainland convent school; because Anton admitted
he had fallen in love with the sixteen year old. A further complication
developed when Anton's father died. Aunt Gail refused to break her period
of mourning, which had been dragging on for two... no four years. Anton
had faithfully mailed a letter to his fiancée every day since she had been
trundled off to school. He envied Anton's assured affection from the young
girl. He prayed Anton would be allowed to marry soon.

Anton said, "I thought you started work with your father on Monday?"

"Yes, yes," Romèe said. "I wouldn't mind trading the life you lead here
for my job with Father. Besides, how much higher do our fortunes have
to rise?"

"Never enough, that's the Laurent motto, No one is ever too rich."

"Or too thin." Romèe continued to follow the progress of the stick of
a girl with her glistening tent of long hair from his vantage point on the
rampart walk overlooking the gates. He liked the way she walked; her
sapling legs easily outdistanced her mother. She constantly danced back
to encourage the older woman up the path's slight incline. All the energy
in the world seemed contained in her lithe movements. Lambs jumped

straight up with the same exuberance and he half expected her to drop the bags she carried to leap for joy. The beaming young woman below shone as if she had discovered a Christmas tree stacked with presents all for her.

The cousins, Romèe and Anton, continued to watch the redhead as she stepped under the shadow of the Artichoke house's second-floor archway which spanned the narrow walk. The mother dropped a suitcase, adjusted her sunglasses, and then ran after her daughter, calling in a desperate tone.

Romèe felt his own heart skip a beat at the hint of doom.

The girl emerged into the sun on the far side of the offending shadow. Joining her, the mother leaned against the stonewall. Instead of retrieving the luggage, the daughter stretched out her arm to point at the wall next to her mother's head.

The older woman jumped a foot, as if expecting to find a lizard next to her ear. Then arms across each other's shoulders, the mother and daughter read the inscription on the weathered stone.

Romèe knew the saying well. "Terribilis est iste locus."

He did not agree Mont Saint Michel was a terrible place. When the place was a prison during the French Revolution, some guard or prisoner could have carved the curse.

Ever since he was thirteen, summer vacations on the Mont had offered up a young damsel determined to woo him. Romèe wanted to find a heart to love for the rest of his life. He recognized contentment in his mother's green eyes. His parents possessed a bond he wanted to emulate. Romèe was convinced his love of the Mont would eventually deliver up his destined, life-long companion. A certain urgency accompanied his search for a potential mate on this final trip. He had graduated from Ann Arbor's business college in the States and summer-long vacations at his aunt's hotel would be shortened to weekends.

Anton and Romèe returned to the hotel through the second floor's back terrace. As the two young men exited the first floor entrance, they nearly knocked over the redhead.

"Can you help us?" she asked. "We're staying here. The Marksteiners?"

"I better retrieve your mother's luggage," Anton said, brushing past the girl on a beeline for the abandoned bag.

As Mrs. Marksteiner spied Anton, she raised her umbrella, thumping him soundly on the shoulder as he stood up with the heavy bag.

"Thief!" she yelled.

"Mother, he is from the hotel!" the girl shouted back.

Romèe cringed. He hated loud women and scenes. He backed into the hotel lobby. The half-door to the office beyond was open. He reached over the small writing desk, unlatched the bottom half of the door and disappeared past the small workplace into his aunt's drawing room. Aunt Gail's rooms were brighter than the outer lobby. The flowered chair near the bay window was softer than he liked.

"Whatever is the racket?" Aunt Gail asked.

"Americans," Romèe explained, watching the melee from the bay window.

Mrs. Marksteiner allowed the battered Anton to carry her bag, explaining her actions while waving the offending umbrella around enough to clip the poor chap across the knees.

"Why don't you rescue your cousin?" Aunt Gail said, peering over his shoulder.

"I should," Romèe said, not moving very quickly to the entrance hallway.

"Catherine." The mirthful chippy was crooning to Anton as she extended her hand. "Mother misunderstood."

"Certainly." Anton bowed crisply, apparently still in pain from the umbrella.

"Marie Marksteiner," Mother said. "Can't be too careful. Are you hurt?" Anton shook his head. "Good," she said. "Any ghosts?"

"What?" Anton lost his polite demeanor.

"Ghosts? Rappings?" The mother persisted.

Romèe unlatched the office's half-door, seeing Catherine blush and diminish in size, as if wishing her skimpy outfit could swallow her. Parents could embarrass you to tears without trying.

"No ghosts to date," Romèe said, picking up two bags in each hand. "I am Romèe Laurent."

Marie Marksteiner grabbed Catherine's shoulder. "St. Joan's mother."

"What?" the young people asked in unison.

"Romèe is the name of Joan of Arc's mother." Mother nodded to each. "This is the place."

"You have a woman's name?" Catherine asked. She stood facing the doorway's sunshine. Widening with the question, her shining green eyes stopped Romèe's answer.

Anton filled in for him, "It is not a feminine or masculine name... more of a destination."

"Yes," Mother said, nearly pushing her daughter aside to look into Romèe's face. "Bound for Rome."

"Not the priesthood," Romèe explained to Catherine over her mother's shoulder. He wanted Catherine to be perfectly clear on that point. Mercy, she could turn a man's mind to mush with those green orbs. "Which room?" he asked Anton.

"Number Three," Anton said. "They have the entire third floor. Would you sign in, Mrs. Marksteiner?"

Catherine carried two smaller shoulder bags up the stairs behind Romèe.

"My mother...," she began in a whisper.

"Is much like all our mothers," Romèe said. He banged the heaviest suitcase into the wall as he smiled at her upturned face. Green eyes like his mother's, and the downfall of all Laurent men.

Catherine continued her sentence. "My mother thinks Joan of Arc is haunting the Mont."

"See there," St. Joan pointed out to Brother Richard.

"Lord, not another one," Brother Richard complained.

"Using the Lord's name?" St. Joan was scandalized. "And you a priest of God's."

"Monk," Brother Richard corrected. "I serve communion. I do not consecrate the host."

"Well, God will forgive you, I suppose." St. Joan danced around Catherine, lifting her long red hair with her invisible fingers.

"They'll notice," Brother Richard cautioned.

"He's too much in love." St. Joan nodded in the direction of Romèe, who was salivating with passion for his destined mate.

"Better give it up," Brother Richard said. "He'll be having her pregnant and occupied with children before she sees a line drawn of your precious Dome."

"Not with me around," St. Joan stood between the couple trying to push Romèe back a step. She wasn't succeeding so she turned her attention on Catherine.

Brother Richard pulled St. Joan to the side. "Leave her alone, at least until your interference can't be witnessed."

"They all take so long," St. Joan complained. "I am losing my patience."

Brother Richard patted her shoulder. "You have never haunted an architect before. I blame myself for advising you to haunt writers. Look at the list. They were all more interested in their own careers than in any message you sent them: Montaigne, Voltaire, Shakespeare, what was his name, or yes Lang. And then there was Sackville-West."

"Not Samuel's mother or Bernard Shaw's wife." St. Joan perched on the pillows in Catherine's intended room.

"True," Brother Richard acknowledged. "However, the French took no notice of your renewed glory."

"Not my glory," St. Joan corrected. "God's glory in saving France for its citizens."

Romèe leaned the suitcases against the banister of the third floor landing while Catherine examined the framed charcoal sketches hung from ceiling to floor on all the walls in the hall.

"All guests," Romèe explained, wanting her to turn her attention back to him.

"Who drew them?" she asked, reading the names of the departed guests.

"Anton is very talented." Romèe was riveted to the wall as she swept a glance in his direction. *My life,* he thought. *I'd give you my life, only keep looking at me.*

Her mother and Anton arrived up the stairs. "No elevator?"

No, Madam." In Romèe's opinion, Anton would have rolled his eyes heavenward if Catherine hadn't been watching him so closely. Anton choked on his words as he unlocked the doors to the suite. "We have tried to maintain the authentic nature of the hotel. It was built in the late seventeen hundreds."

"The hike is good for you, us." Catherine smiled at Anton.

'Meant for me, 'Romèe complained in his soul at the misdirected smile.

Catherine did then turn in his direction, briefly. "Romèe was bragging about your art."

'Bragging,' Romèe had never been accused of that before, but he forgave her. The sound of his name in the silken timbre of her voice warmed his blood.

In an off-hand tone Anton offered, "I sketch all my guests."

"He compared you to Botticelli's redheaded models." Romèe claimed his tongue again and Catherine's focus for a minute.

"Do you also paint?" her mother asked Anton.

"No," Anton said, as he opened the white drapes in the ivy-decorated room. "I'm content with my pencils."

Catherine stepped into the second room. "Is this the Queen of Hearts room?"

"Absolutely." Romèe followed on her heels. He almost added the bedroom was decorated for Anton's fiancée, but he did *not* want to bring his cousin's name back into the conversation.

"Anton," her mother called. "Catherine is going to architectural school."

"Bragging," Catherine said to Romèe and then blushed. She stepped back into the foyer.

St. Joan embraced Catherine so quickly Brother Richard could only grab the bottom edge of her golden tunic of linked mail before the Saint disappeared into Catherine's slim bones. He wound one of his bare feet around the banister's post determined to yank St. Joan out of Catherine's body as soon as he could.

Romèe followed Catherine out to the landing. His body felt pulled to her side as if the secrets of the universe were contained in her soul. He scolded himself for his lack of nonchalance. He knew nothing about her or her family. All he knew was how he felt.

Catherine's voice dropped an octave and with a stiffened manner, as if surprised at her own request, she asked Anton, "May I borrow a few of your pencils?"

Brother Richard's ghost fell to the floor as St. Joan exited the door between Catherine's bones. "I told you, Saint Peter specifically forbids you to inhabit any more souls."

"I only touched her tongue," St. Joan said, defensively. "I never broke the seal of her soul."

Brother Richard stamped his bare foot. "You know you impart too much courage into people. They think they're invincible. Think of poor Evita, gone before she should have been called naturally."

St. Joan hung her head. She played with a singed piece of her hair near her ear. "I need more patience."

"The Lord gives us all the time we need," Brother Richard reminded her.

Reclaiming her guile, Catherine said sweetly, "I've only brought a camera, and I want to outline my own rendition of Mont Saint Michel."

Her mother interrupted. "Could I pay you for a sketch pad, too?"

"Of course not," Anton said. "I'll be delighted to offer you some of my tools."

'Good old Anton,' Romèe thought. A French gentleman to his last clean handkerchief. But, Anton quickly descended the steps. Too quickly. Mrs. Marksteiner and Catherine stared after him. Romèe coughed to cover Anton's rude exit. "He's probably fetching the pencils right now," Romèe said to disguise his cousin's bad manners. "We hope your stay will be a pleasant one." Romèe couldn't let go of his place on Catherine's floor, so he asked. "Which of these bags should I bring to your room?'

Her mother pointed to the heaviest. "Catherine's," she said. "Summer reading. Remember, Catherine, you promised to read about St. Joan haunting writers?"

Romèe lifted the cumbersome suitcase. "How many books are in here?"

"Leave it just inside the door," Catherine said.

"About a dozen," her mother said. "I only brought material about Bernard Shaw and Samuel Clemens. However, authors from Shakespeare, Voltaire and Anatole France have documented fixations, if not actual hauntings by St. Joan."

"Shaw did write a play about a ghostly vision, didn't he?" Romèe watched Catherine turn away, but he did remember reading such a play. He was not just trying to please her mother. It was time to leave. "Could I interest you in a tour?" he asked. "Or could I show you a nice restaurant for lunch?"

Her mother patted his back as if she understood his reluctance to leave her beautiful daughter. "Give us an hour to unpack and stretch out for a minute."

"Of course," Romèe said, his hand on the banister held onto some hope.

"I'll be right down," Catherine said. Romèe heard her continue to speak to her mother as he slowly went down the steps. "Whatever possessed me to ask for Anton's sketching equipment?"

"They're both happy to oblige. Don't you want to unpack?"

"No. I'm gone," Catherine said, heading towards the steps.

Romèe hurried into the street so he wouldn't be tempted to eavesdrop. Catherine flew out the door behind him. "I could eat."

Romèe laughed in relief. All to himself. He had her all to himself! His knees were weak, so he pointed out the restaurant across from the hotel's door. "Is this close enough?"

She jumped up and kissed his cheek without touching him anywhere else. "Yes," she said and then had to drag his stricken hide to a table.

Seated under the awning trellis of fragrant pink roses, Romèe swore he believed in love at first sight. He tasted the coffee and let his fork play with the food in his plate. His nostrils cleared with the coffee's aroma. The sweet scent of the hanging garden dissipated for an instant of saneness. His mother and father's love story proved knowing whom you loved the first time you saw them did happen.

Catherine had kissed him, but on the cheek like some younger brother of Anton's. If his eyes were not black, Romèe was sure the jealous monster coming to life inside him, would change his eye color to match hers in shades of green envy. Nevertheless, he wasn't ready to throw in the towel. Anton was taken; Romèe on the other hand was not.

After devouring two croissants, shrimp salad, a nice steak with no French fries, and two pieces of pie, which counted his own untouched piece, Catherine was ready to stop talking about her mother.

"All her husbands died?" Romèe just wanted to keep her talking, facing in his general direction. He enjoyed looking at her face, her quick change of expressions, her perky mouth, her great ocean-deep eyes. She was all he needed in his life, exactly all.

"Mother's not a good cook," Catherine said and giggled at the face he must have made. Then she changed her demeanor to serious. "Daddy died of a heart attack when I was ten. I still miss him."

Romèe resisted the urge to wrap his arms around her to comfort her. He moved his chair closer to her side of the table, in case the opportunity presented itself again. "And the others?" he asked, grateful to the Lord for her continued presence.

"Well, George left so she divorced him. Actually, she told him to get out. She thought he was a letch."

"A letch?" Romèe grasped the meaning of the word, but most wives did not describe their husbands as lechers.

"Mother said she caught a look in his eyes when I was swimming one day."

"I see," Romèe said, his blood reacting in anger to the brute. "Your mother knows best."

"Yes," Catherine said. "Jimmy Marksteiner was a good substitute father. He died in October. Mother became engaged to his lawyer, Danny Passantino, in February. They're getting married the end of June when we get home."

"They were friends," Romèe said. 'Home. Of course, she would leave.' "Don't you like it here?" he asked, crazy with love.

"I do, but doesn't Mother remind you of a praying mantis who eats her mates?"

"Of course not!" Romèe defended the woman. "Anton's mother should take a lesson from her."

"How so?" Catherine seemed to concentrate too intensely on Romèe impending answer.

"She's widowed," Romèe explained, not without wondering if this sudden interest was for Anton's sake. "...in mourning for nearly four years now. Anton can't..."

"I know how Anton feels," Catherine interrupted. "You're right. Mother always says life is for the living. Let's walk up to the top of the monastery."

Romèe laid too much money on the table as he struggled to follow her quick departure.

"Tell me everything you know about the Mont," Catherine said, as he caught up to her.

Romèe's role as tour guide demanded he not notice Catherine only came up to the second button on his shirt, or that his arms were double the size of hers. He could not find his tongue, for pity sake.

12

Catherine chatted away, "It was called Mont Tombe in 708 when St. Aubert dreamed of Saint Michael. I wonder if Joan of Arc was dozing when she first saw him?"

Romèe recovered enough to say, "Without the constant entertainment of television, we might all be inspired by visions." He brushed aside the crush of vendors, pointing toward the marsh grasses. "In 709 they say the coast sank inundating the forest of Scissy which originally surrounded the Mont."

Catherine said, "When the monks returned from a year-long trek for holy relics to sanctify the church, they were surprised to find the trees had vanished. When the trees were used to build the Abbey, the soil was washed away."

Catherine's knowledge of the Mont surprised Romèe. He reached for Catherine's hand but she extended it toward a bald vendor's rack of rainbow scarves. "Mont Saint Michel doesn't seem in peril of the sea today, does it? Have you been here before?" He would have remembered this sprite, even years ago.

"No. Just read about it. Mother usually packs a ton of books for each vacation. I helped her out by reading as many histories of the Mont and Joan of Arc's trial as I could before we left Ann Arbor."

"I graduated in May from the University of Michigan." Romèe gripped her shoulder. "We were in the same town and never met?"

Catherine patted his arm. "The campus is rather large."

Romèe agreed. "Business school is on the main campus."

Catherine nodded. "Mother and I are having our last vacation together, before she re-marries again. I've been accepted as a student at the architectural school in Lansing." Catherine shook her head as if to clear her mind of troubling thoughts. "Mother's sure St. Joan made a pilgrimage here after the siege of Paris, when her voices seemed to desert her."

Romèe offered, "The Pucelle of Orleans was missing for four months before she was taken into custody."

13

St. Joan breathed a fact into her gallant's ear.

Romèe rumpled his hair, a habit he wanted to quit. "I suppose it's possible Joan of Arc brought captured English artillery to help defend the Mont."

Catherine said, "She traveled at night from Vaucoulers to the dauphin in Chinon in eleven days." Catherine skipped up a step to the entrance of an art gallery. From her elevated position she placed an innocent hand on her devoted knight's shoulder. "You know a lot about Joan of Arc." Romèe would have knelt and asked for her betrothal right then, but Catherine patted his cheek, breaking the spell. "Mother says the French have forgotten her." Catherine continued her progress up the hill. "Tell me more about the Mont."

"This is my last summer here, too," Romèe said. "My father has a job for me in New York."

"Too bad," she said.

"I'd like to live here," Romèe said.

"Me, too." Catherine stopped so quickly he almost collided with her. "I wonder if Joan of Arc thought about living here after the war was over. What did the Abbey look like if she visited in 1430?"

"I don't know," Romèe said. "The dates are confusing. The Merveille was supposedly planned in 1203. The Roman Choir collapsed in 1421, during the Hundred Years War, which started in 1386. Cardinal Louis d'Estouteville commanded the 119 defending knights and rebuilt the church between 1446 and 1521."

"That was after they burnt Joan in 1431," Catherine mused. "King Charles probably donated funds to rebuild the church. Without the Merveille towers, the church might have resembled a loaf of bread."

The rest of the trip up the winding path and steps to the Abbey was a blur to Romèe. She was the one. Before him cavorted his future bride. He hoped his incessant smile didn't convince her he was an idiot. Romèe could see the two of them living together in maybe the Artichoke house, with children. He needed to speak to his parents about his plans to stay on the Mont.

The coolness of the air conditioning added to the crisp cleanliness of the Queen-of-Heart's suite. Catherine reached out to touch the muslin draperies that hung around and over the four-poster bed, but withdrew her hand. She needed a shower. The June heat and the grubby tourists, who were wont to collide with her on the way down from the impressive, high-vaulted church, made Catherine feel laden with germs.

Catherine looked at the row of books her mother had unpacked. Between the door to the landing and the bathroom, a dozen tomes awaited her perusal. One was a photograph album of the Mont that Danny assembled after his trip in 1995. Catherine placed it on the white bedspread along with a guidebook from the same year.

Catherine's clothes were hung neatly in the closet. From the muffled snores she could hear on the other side of the connecting bathroom, she could tell Mother was exhausted from unpacking.

In the tepid shower with her soapy hair hanging down in front of her face, Catherine analyzed Anton's interest in her. According to Romèe, Anton thought her hair classified her as a Botticelli model. The younger Romèe was sweet, but Anton was the man. Her hands stopped in their ritual of cleanliness. Wouldn't it be great to stay here, live here like Anton? Forget college. Catherine wanted to stay on the miniature island. If someone could provide a corner of some room, she would be content. Anton was the only way. His mother owned the hotel. Romèe had a job in New York; he'd be out of the picture soon.

Towel drying her hair in front of the old-fashioned, pedestal mirror, Catherine heard a slight rustle outside her door. She wrapped another towel around herself, and towel-turban in place, opened the door to find a sketchpad with pencils, but no Anton.

Catherine mounted the bed with the pencils and pad.

St. Joan motioned for Brother Richard to come closer. "Now is the time."

"Do not inhabit the child again, or I will leave." Brother Richard crossed his arms to confirm his resolve.

"May I at least guide her arm?" St. Joan pleaded.

"Promise?" Brother Richard stood guard.

What was this sudden urge to draw? Catherine needed to show Anton they had something in common. But a creepy feeling tingled up her right arm, as if someone were blowing hot air on her skin. Catherine took the towel off her head and rubbed her arm with the rough cotton. Her limb still tingled but at least nothing was crawling on her. She lifted her damp hair from her shoulders, rested her back on the soft, dry pillows, and let her hair spill over the top of the high cushions.

Catherine opened the guidebook written by the curator of the Mont, but curiously published in Florence. She selected a page that showed the details of the Mont's construction and propped it open with the help of a small lacey bolster. With the sketchpad balanced on her knees, Catherine began to draft what she remembered of the empty west platform in front of the Abbey doors where an older section of the cathedral had fallen. Catherine felt drowsy, confused. She checked the clock on the bedside table: 2:00.

Catherine's arm seemed disembodied from her lazy self as it arched over the pad, the pencil busy with its lines of remembrance.

Catherine slept and the pencil moved on.

***

The ghost of St. Joan was entirely pleased. Here was a perfect tool, this silly girl with hair longer than it had a right to be. St. Joan touched her own cropped locks. She went to the mirror, but no reflection appeared.

"Never mind," Brother Richard said. "Your hair needed to be short for easy placement of your helmet."

"Yes," St. Joan said, "But where is my battle helmet now?"

"The wars are over for you," her confessor said.

St. Joan still wore the golden links of her protective mail over a short tunic. Her leggings suited the after-life, even though skirts didn't hamper getting around anymore. "I miss the horses from the campaign," St. Joan said.

"They await you in the Elysian Fields of heaven," Brother Richard promised.

"Riding them seems an ungracious act now," St. Joan mused, "to ask another being to carry you."

St. Joan appraised a finished sketch and turned the page for the sleeping architect. One more drawing of the silhouette of the island was needed, maybe with the sun or moon rising over the empty platform to hint at the pink crystal dome that St. Joan planned to have built at Mont Saint Michel.

"The French keep forgetting their Maid of Orleans," Brother Richard encouraged. "The virgin who had, after all, saved their nation."

"They remain intent on celebrating that grandiose butcher, Napoleon." St. Joan frowned.

"The Dome of St. Joan will bring France back to its humble and miraculous origins," Brother Richard counseled, "when God found them beaten and instilled a genetic pride in their patriotic molecules."

Catherine's mother stirred in the next room.

St. Joan closed the book of her dream edifice, relaxing Catherine's hand. The spent pencil rolled off the bed. The spirit lines drawn with Catherine's appropriated arm started to fade. The Maid of Orleans grew sad.

She had once nerved the dauphin and his advisors to fight as a French nation against the English crown, only to see their resolve weaken…just as the faint lines of her magnificent Dome now dimmed on Catherine's sketchpad.

However, giving up was not a phrase familiar to St. Joan.

CHAPTER TWO

New York City

In the early New York spring afternoon, eight-foot high rosewood doors stood sentinel. Their curved brass handles promised a certain coldness. Romèe looked at his tardy watch which he kept on the Mont's time schedule: 4:00. He turned his head searching for a sign from his father's secretary. She noticed his hesitation, cocked her head quizzically and waved at him to go in. The doors opened without his touch. There stood his father eye-to-eye with him.

Mr. Laurent dropped his arms from the doors and embraced his son. "Welcome to the fleet."

"Yes, Father."

His father released him and they entered the shipping office.

The ships in the fleet were not beauties. Oil barges tended to be ugly, slow-moving beasts. Romèe headed for the windows. The office did not suggest his father was a tyrant. The desk sat on the right side of the room, a table really. Lounge chairs were grouped near the fireplace on the left. Most executives sat with their backs to the windows so the expressions of visitors were highlighted, leaving the manager's face inscrutable, hidden in the shadows. Romèe's father refused to play competitive games. He insisted on good service and honesty. 'Trust.' Romèe heard ringing in his head as he reached the French doors to the balcony. Business was based on trust.

"Is my sister still holding off on the wedding?" His father asked.

Romèe nodded, not opening the beveled-glass paned doors. He did not appreciate any vista not from the Mont. After the panoramic expanse of heavens surrounding Mont Saint Michel skies elsewhere seemed crowded. One-dimensional glimpses of blue seen between buildings or trees harked back to mere paintings or post-cards. Only on the Mont did he realize the infinite universe and his humble place in the scheme of things. "I'd rather not start tomorrow."

Romèe turned to face his father.

Seated at the table, Father looked up from his pen. "What's that?" Romèe shifted in his shoes, and then walked to the fireplace. His father joined him. "Sit down, son. Tell me what's bothering you."

Romèe sat and rested his elbows on the arms of the chair. He ran his hands through his curls. "Why do we have to keep making more money?"

Father opened the lid of a box of cigars and then closed the ornate box. "We have enough. It grows on its own."

"I'm not sure you should count on me." Romèe stopped rumpling his hair, conscious of the wreck he had made of his appearance. As Romèe tried to smooth his hair back down, his father smiled slightly. Romèe moved to the edge of his chair. "I don't know what I want."

Father's smile flirted with his mouth. "You could start here, go to the Brazil office, and when you figure out what you want, do that."

"No." Romèe escaped the bounds of the chair. "I love you and want to please you, but...." Romèe paced the floor, kicking at the lush carpet. He rejoined his father, sitting down quietly. "I'm a nut case."

"You're young." Father leaned forward to pat his son's knee. "The whole world awaits you. Getting started seems like a final decision."

"Exactly!" Romèe was on his feet again for a second, then he slumped down in the chair, feeling defeated.

"Why don't we wait a year?" Father suggested. Romèe brightened. "A tour of the continent, the English islands, Ireland, Scotland..." Romèe was surprised to find himself positively smiling. His father smiled broadly, too. "Maybe Italy, India?"

Romèe frowned. "The Mont. I want to stay on the Mont. Aunt Gail will have me." He noticed his father lacked any enthusiasm for the idea. "I found a green-eyed girl."

"Oh," His father nodded at the new information.

"Mother's eyes," Romèe said, idiotically. "She's studying to be an architect."

"All the more reason to tour Europe."

Romèe shook his head no. "Her name is Catherine. On the plane here, I nodded off and dreamt about a short dark-skinned girl about Catherine's age. A Lorraine peasant girl? She was talking to herself, but she didn't hold a phone. I couldn't make out what she was saying, but I knew it was important. In the dream, I'm hiding behind a huge tree. She had knelt down in front of the tree. Maybe she was praying."

"Not to the tree," Father said.

"She faced away from the tree," Romèe said. "That's why I couldn't hear her."

Father clapped his hands. "I think Joan of Arc was the girl you saw."

"Catherine's mother wants to find the ghost of St. Joan on Mont Saint Michel."

"How does this fit into your plans?"

"Could the Saint haunt both Catherine and me?" The words reformed in Romèe's brain after he heard them with his own ears. With renewed confidence, he told his father, "I feel I should be there to help Catherine. She's dazzling."

"The avatar," His father said. "The Pucelle de Diu is the most romantic ideal in history."

"I meant Catherine. She's been accepted as a graduate student at Lansing's architectural school." Romèe followed his father to the door.

"Would she like a tour of the continent before she starts her classes?" Father asked, loud enough for his secretary to hear.

"I've not said more than two words to her." Romèe added with his back to the secretary, "Tell Mother about Catherine's green eyes."

"I most certainly will." Father patted his back. "Now, take your time, son, and find out about the trip. Miss Jackson here will be happy to arrange everything."

Romèe watched them as the elevator doors closed on the plush outer office. He heard his father say, "Separate rooms, of course."

Mont Saint Michel

At midnight on the Marksteiners' first evening in Mont Saint Michel, something was certainly throwing itself against the third floor windows in Mother's room at the Hotel de' Bermont.

"Bats," Gail Bermont, the hotel owner, called the third floor racket. The gray-haired woman assured Catherine that the full moon's reflection attracted them, that the glass wouldn't break.

"Is the porter, Romèe, in?" Catherine asked.

"My nephew flew to New York this afternoon, but my son is here." She called back over her shoulder to Anton.

The fluorescent lights in the office ceiling sent rainbows down each translucent strand in the woman's thick hair, but Catherine couldn't find a line of age on her face. Her blue eyes widened when she introduced herself. Gail Bermont showed no sign of vexation at the evening's interruption or suspicion. Instead, her eyes thirsted for input.

Catherine was sure Mrs. Bermont knew the color of her socks, even as she stood barefoot on the terrazzo tile of the entrance hall.

Romèe gone to work in New York, already? She'd barely said hello to him. She'd thought they were friends. Further piqued at the landlady's quick dismissal of her fears Catherine argued with her; "The moon can't change the behavior of bats. They don't use their eyes to fly."

Without a shirt on, Anton poked his head around the living quarter's door. "Satellite dishes short-circuit the bats' radar. The same kinetic, electronic energy involved can blind humans."

"Nonsense," Catherine said, but smiled at her view of him. Curly blond hairs on Anton's chest gathered around his nipples. Each muscle was highlighted with the fluffy hair. He raised his hand to his curls and pulled on the thick crown, as if to keep himself awake. The line of hair collecting from his navel to his pajama bottoms doubled in production.

Catherine wanted to nestle in the soft hair of this man. Then Anton crossed his arms, hiding great fields of flesh and curl. Catherine raised her eyes to his face, wondering if he'd noticed her concentration.

He said, "Candles will cut down the reflected image of the moon."

As Anton drew away from the half-door desk, Catherine reached to touch his woolly back. He stepped across the room to a low credenza and retrieved a box of candles from its bottom shelf. Bodies need hands the way wet clay demands shaping. The Lord was good to make men so pleasurably contoured. Heaven couldn't be much without the pleasure of touch. Anton could have her favorite green floppy hat and the book of drawings by Leonardo da Vinci, if he'd allow her to test his mettle with her fingertips.

Catherine let herself imagine falling down into the barrel of Anton's soul. She lingered in the sleepy grip of her desire, repeating her dilemma, "It's like a Dracula movie up there, in Mother's room."

But as Anton closed the upper half of the door, he only said, "The candles will help."

Catherine touched the cold wall of the stairwell and tapped her toes against the front of each step. Her stomach lurched as she imagined stumbling backwards.

When Romèe carried their bags up earlier, he continually banged into the narrow walls. Did his body hair match his dark head of curls? Had she caught a hint of interest in his black eyes, when he'd commiserated with her about her crazy mother? It didn't matter now. He was gone from the Mont.

Catherine suppressed a cough as she searched for a light switch at the top of the stairs. In order to breathe properly, she needed space to stretch. She found the switch plate which had been wallpapered over not to break the lines of the green-and-white striped hall. When had Mont Saint Michel turned into such a scary place? When they walked up to the hotel, the shadow from the Artichoke house spanning the walk had frightened Mother. Then Catherine was sorry she had spooked Mother again by pointing past her head to the Latin words etched in the stone, 'Terrible is this place.'

Catherine's enchanted, dream-island vacation for budding architects began as a nightmare with the warning. The wretched reality of houses strewn at the foot of the ill-conceived church, whose foundations tottered at each strike of lightning and where the lake of tranquility had turned into a grass-growing mud fill -- the reality had dampened Catherine's earlier fascination with the island fortress.

She had envisioned lemon-scented, cobblestone paths, where processions of silk-gowned clerics and wedding guests tread among flowers-strewn walks to the immaculate abbey. Catherine expected brilliant swans on the blue lagoon surrounding the mystic isle; instead the gray, mold-begotten tourist cages crept all the way up to the rock-pile of a church that barely stood upright.

Even the bright and constant smile of Romèe couldn't diminish her disappointment. Catherine thumped on the wall next to her mother's door. Sturdy enough. No sense scaring Mother more than those blood-hungry things on the other side of the rickety, diamond-shaped casements were already doing.

In Mother's room, flapping noises continued to attack the glass. Catherine said, "Anton, without a shirt on, said candles diminish the moon's attraction."

"Shirt or not," Mother agreed with Anton.

The wings of something swished against the black panes as if to challenge the brightness. As she approached the windows with the candles, Catherine's replica surprised her. Fright made her cheekbones more prominent and her jaw jutted forward from clenching her teeth. She glanced at her mirrored image back to her mother, who appeared merely curious.

Anton gained a point. The shapeless things buffeting the panes ceased as the candles shifted the outer glow of the moon.

Catching her mother's hand as she started to pull open one of the windows, Catherine warned, "They might come back."

But when Catherine let go, Mother opened the window with a jerk.

A cloud of white feathers or blossoms sailed into the room. The noise hadn't been bats. Mother picked up the fallen flowers.

"Fluers de lis," Mother said, "lilies from St. Joan."

After Catherine and Mother rescued each lily petal from St. Joan and pressed them between acid-free pages of Francis Gies' Joan of Arc published in 1924, Mother stacked four books on top of the bulging volume to press the flowers flat. Out of chronological order, Catherine read the titles: the 1918 Joan of Arc, by Lucky Foster Madison, Sackville-West's 1936 Saint Joan of Arc, Bernard Shaw's 1926 six scene play, Saint Joan, and, of course, Samuel Clemens' 1924 Joan of Arc.

Mother climbed into the bed and Catherine got comfortable with the ivy-decorated bedspread over her shoulders. Although Catherine was interested in its architecture, Mother's fixation to find the spirit of Joan of

Arc at the Mont had initiated their trip. With this new affirmation for her quest, Catherine expected Mother to recount for the hundredth time all the stories about St. Joan haunting authors, which she did. "When he was a boy, Samuel Clemons caught a page of a book as it blew across his path in Hannibal, Missouri," Mother started the rendition as if Catherine were five and asking for her favorite bedtime story.

"Twain rushed home to ask his mother if Joan of Arc ever lived," Catherine finished the tale.

Mother continued, "He was so excited to find the heroine was real, he determined to become a writer."

Catherine yawned. "He later wrote about St. Joan with such convincing passion his daughters testified to weeping with him whenever he read the last chapter. If you stopped talking about St. Joan for five minutes, I wouldn't keep dreaming what you want to be experiencing for yourself."

Mother didn't miss a beat. "Joan of Arc demands recognition."

Romèe had blinked his lush, dark lashes politely when Catherine told him Mother expected to recognize Joan's spirit floating down one of the Abbey's ancient corridors. Romèe was certainly an odd name. Not many boys she knew in America would sit still for that moniker.

She broached the subject of staying on the Mont without benefit of college. "Anton lives in the hotel with his mother."

"It's a nice business for a family."

"He did leave a sketch pad and pencils outside my door, even after you whacked him soundly on the head and shoulders."

"Actually, one shoulder and his knees." Mother raised herself to her elbows, pounded the pillows and gave Catherine the benefit of her sporadic psychic vision. "I don't feel anything negative toward the young man." Then she apologized, "I'm not being honest." Mother nodded to herself. "I feel a strong sense of danger, no not danger; it's more like a reason for feeling protective." Mother tugged at her hair in a distracted manner as if she were pulling ideas out of the white reservoir of curls. "He's in love with the woman he's going to marry."

Catherine brightened considerably.

But Mother noticed the ambiguity in her statement and reached for Catherine as if to rescue her from the edge of a precipice. "You're more beautiful and taller."

Accustomed to her mother's dramatics, Catherine asked, "Can you actually see who he's interested in?"

Mother shook her head and mumbled something about nobody's daughter, nearly rubbing the skin off her forehead to get a clearer picture. "She's dark."

The term 'nobody's daughter' dampened Catherine's eyes. "Without a mother in the house 'nobody's daughter' could refer to me after you marry."

"While I yet breathe you are my daughter." Mother raised her voice. "Roofs don't hold families, hearts do."

Catherine hugged her mother and kissed her brow. "I'll be careful. Remember telling me hearts may refuse to love twice? After three husbands, you haven't slowed down. You still opened your heart to Danny."

Mother cheered up at the mention of Danny. "You're a good girl."

"I might ask Anton to take me to the highest portals in the cathedral," Catherine said to show that her interest in Anton was professional—sort of. She immersed herself in the imagined spectacle. Saint Michael himself perched golden on the steeple would have to share her view. Flinging the coverlet off, she jumped to the floor, imitating a bird soaring over the tiny island. "I will see the stair steps among the pinnacles of the Merveille and all the secret patios and roof gardens of the residents."

While Catherine described her photographic plan, Mother began to yawn. Catherine blew out the magic candles and headed toward her own bed, content with the planned tour of Mont Saint Michel.

She checked on her mother from the doorway of the connecting bathroom. Mother had sunk lower in her pillows. Her feathery, ash-white hair gentled her features. Catherine stared for a moment trying to pinpoint the family resemblance everyone commented on. The nose was exactly hers, but Mother's eyes were close to the bridge of her nose while Catherine's were widely spaced. And her mother's brow hung over the eye cavity while Catherine's sloped up and away.

The majority of Catherine's features seemed delivered from her father. She hoped her jaw line would not soften as her mother's had. Catherine stretched up behind her ears thinking her neck must be twice as long as her mother's. Do necks shrink? Probably, yes, the soft cartilage must harden and become less elastic. She promised herself to keep her neck stretched long, so that at fifty she could still measure a hand's breadth between her ears and shoulders. Was she measuring a racehorse, how many hands high?

Closing her eyes, Catherine knew she would be able to draw buildings for the rest of her life if she could master the imperfections and beauties of the Mont's architecture.

Her first dream was of a gigantic pink diamond on her own hand. As she looked closely at its intricate facets, she could see hanging gardens, festooned arches, and blue butterflies floating within its boundaries. Catherine settled softly down with a few of the butterflies to the grassy floor of the dreamscape, where a young girl picked flowers for wreaths and garlands to hang on the branches of a sacred beech tree. Sweet orisons wafted through the air. Catherine recognized the gentle maid who became the champion of France.

"Joan of Arc," she called.

The girl dropped to her knees, holding up her hands to the butterflies, as Catherine sped away to her own pristine bed.

Catherine woke slightly and pondered Mother's other world of spirits; specifically how time-lines did not intervene in their visits. History and the future intertwined in the very strands of Catherine's red hair. Earlier dreams had allowed Catherine to see her children's freckled faces before she even considered mating and her death before she felt any fear of dying.

A floating feeling lingered as sleep pulled out Catherine's hooks on reality. Sure enough, she watched the eastern horizon from her favorite bedroom chair in Ann Arbor. Something was coming from a long way off to overwhelm everything. Change was the result but loss would be its tool. She tried to discern the epicenter of the unkind force stretching from north to south. One wall of white dust not as high as the moon approached. The massive state of the premonition urged her to warn everyone. In her dream she ran around knocking on strange doors telling Romèe to hoard toilet paper and Anton to buy ten years supply of insulin and birth control pills. Her youthful Eden had disappeared.

Catherine fought the paralysis of sleep but reached another level of her soul-brain, where glass structures rose precariously above ruins of massive, old wooden beams and stone blocks. Flexible translucent panels replaced masonry to reach efficiently for the unfailing sun. Rest came for a few minutes.

Then some mouse out in Hotel de Bermont's hall or deep in the attic busily ate his crackers or walnuts. Catherine fought not to hear the crunching. She pictured the pristine glass walls of her earlier dream crumbling under the weight of mighty teeth. Something bigger than Michigan was swallowing cities. People clung to its molars, slipped between the gray eyeteeth. The monster's hunger knew no appeasement. Catherine smelled mold on the green cloud of breath, which escaped when the thing opened its mouth to consume her. The world vanished into itself, as Gog and Magog re-muddied their empire.

CHAPTER THREE

Sunday, June 2nd

Hearing her mother move around in the next room, Catherine slipped out of bed. Mother tiptoed into the room; because she'd worn high heels for so long her arches demanded the tensed position. Her shoulders reached for the familiar height heels provided, just as dieters' stomachs demand girth when the fat is gone. The conscious effort needed for her mother's heels to touch the cold floor would be required for thinning people to imagine the direction of their backbones, instead of protruding their navels out to lost dimensions.

Catherine said, "I dreamt Mont Saint Michel was about to grind me up."

"An architect's dream." Mother sat on one foot in the dark red, wingback chair draping her free leg over her knee.

The test of love, according to Mother's teaching, was to encourage the highest aspirations of others. Catherine perched on the footstool and recounted all she could about her dream of the Maid.

"I hate competing with my own daughter for a haunting," Mother said.

Catherine explained the dream again because Mother had obviously not heard how the dream started. "The pink diamond on my hand means someone on the Mont will ask to marry me."

Mother scoffed, "Anton, that porter?"

"Owner's son is his correct title. I like blond men."

Mother switched topics to Joan of Arc's involvement in the rites of spring. She mentioned the history of pagan religions from *The Golden*

Bough. "Trees were thought to be sacred beings and young virgins decorated their branches with wreaths of flowers getting intoxicated by the aroma." Mother reached her hand out, lifting a long strand of Catherine's hair examining the ends for split-end damage. "Which made it easier for young men to seduce them."

"Don't worry. I don't need perfume to heighten my interest in men. As you always tell me, my hormones are raging. Anton could make me Queen of the Mont."

But Mother was too engrossed in her favorite obsession to comment on her daughter staying permanently on the Mont. "When Joan of Arc was visited by you, she might have mistaken your astral-projection for one of her Voices. The whole sequence of events causing a maid of France to believe she was singled out to lead an army to save her country could have been triggered by you." Catherine started to rise, but Mother pushed her back down on the stool. "Knowing St. Joan's greatness and destiny and the respectful tone in your voice of historic recognition, could have passed the confidence you felt directly to the future Saint."

Catherine stayed with the outrageous thought for only a moment. "What about my vision of the glass dome that the pink ring let me slip into? Where the fallen part of the oldest section of the Abbey used to be, on the west terrace, the Dome rose up into the Merveille towers, snug in its facets. The new glass dome provided room for a greenhouse and a butterfly haven."

Mother glommed onto the butterflies. "Folk legends tell of butterflies accompanying the banners of St. Joan as she rode into battle." Then Mother touched Catherine's shoulder to punctuate the most important message of the dream. "Joan of Arc has chosen you, my promising architect, to envision the perfect edifice to bring her glory back into the heart of the French people. You will design that glass dome for Mont Saint Michel to hold her name ensconced in the heights of heaven."

St. Joan kissed the older woman's right cheekbone. Brother Richard made a nervous sign of the cross with his eyes rolled up toward the helpful heavenly hosts.

Catherine doubted. "Design the dome? I don't have my degree, or any connections to receive such an assignment from the Church, or the government."

"But the idea is yours." Mother rubbed the point where St. Joan had placed a grateful kiss. "And, it came straight from Joan of Arc. She knows your future greatness just as you knew her history. "She'll give you all the details."

After a leisurely morning shower, Catherine surveyed her body in the room's oval pedestal mirror. Would a career as an architect add to her boney attractiveness? She needed to dress in an outfit to charm the dull crust out of every eye, maybe just Anton's for today. Catherine slipped on her jeans and grabbed a sweatshirt. Coffee might be perking across the street at the cafe. As she opened the door she nearly stepped on a tray holding croissants and a thermos of coffee, compliments of Hotel de' Bermont.

Catherine took off her foraging outfit and, cup-in-hand, returned to the mirror for another assessment. Her ears were small. Maybe this was the face she would consider at fifty. She pulled on her ear lobe. Was that the last visage of baby opulence, begging to be nibbled by a mature male? Her mouth, while a bit wide, presented an expectant expression as if a heavy, fresh peach was being sliced and offered slowly enough for her saliva glands to quicken at the expected pleasure. Although they were pale green, her eyes did project a sense of pride. A glint of curiosity shone from a brain able to affix immediate, if even wrong, judgments. Blood pulsed to her white-nailed fingertips and her toes curled in narcissistic pleasure.

Worldwide renown would do. Structures in India, Rome, Paris, New York and Argentina would rise to call forth the acclaim of her early admirers and late critics. The possible seemed inevitable.

In the meantime, she'd busy herself trying on outfits for the tour with Anton. Catherine started with a black athletic bra and bikini pants, then poured her hips into a black leather skirt. Over short, black socks she tied up angle-high boots. A black lace blouse and a studded black barrette to pin up all her hair added to the look. She scowled and stomped around the room before re-approaching the mirror. A sudden chill, as she viewed the black-stony outfit, summoned the crunching monster dream.

She switched the lace shell for a yellow blouse before the coldness left. Instead of re-hanging the leather skirt she dropped it in the wastebasket, glad to be rid of its dampening effect. Catherine slipped on her safe jeans and raced down the steps to capture Anton.

Anton stood with a knee cocked, his foot balanced against the doorframe of the hotel's entrance. The street's brightness presented a Fifties silhouette of his tight jeans, high-collared shirt and smart cap. Anton stepped backward into the street when he saw her. Catherine's heart skipped. His eyes were light blue and the effort to focus left them watery.

"Are you free to show me the Mont?" Catherine asked.

"Romèe said he gave you a tour." Anton's attention was glued to the approaching postman.

"And thank you for the sketch pad."

"Did you use it, then?" Anton tipped the man who handed him one letter, which he immediately tore open, mumbling an apology as he read it quickly.

"I think I fell asleep," Catherine answered, not actually remembering where she put the sketchpad. "Will you show me how to get into the bell tower?"

"I'll be glad to," Anton tucked the finished letter into his vest pocket. "May I carry some of your camera equipment?" He checked his watch. "10:00 o'clock. Mr. Bellefleur is punctual enough to set your watch. But, I'm afraid the clouds are gathering for a storm."

In thanks for burdening himself with her equipment, Catherine displayed her most alluring smile, which Anton missed as he reset the shoulder strap on the carrier. "Hold still," Catherine said as she adjusted the camera's focus, giving him another opportunity to appreciate her smile. "I need a picture of my tour guide."

Romèe inserted his face close to the lens. "You mean me?"

She laughed. "Yes, Yes. Get shoulder to shoulder with your cousin. I'll immortalize the both of you."

"Romèe," Anton seemed too relieved, "show this young beauty the trap door to the bell tower."

"No way," Catherine said. "He tells me nothing, lets everybody knock into me, and just grins away. Anton, have mercy. You're the citizen here."

Romèe's grin confirmed the basis of her plea.

"All right," Anton said. "I see the problem, but he can carry the bag."

"Absolutely," Romèe said.

"I thought you went back to the mainland," Catherine said. "I asked for you last night."

Romèe froze. "What happened? My father gave me a reprieve from the shipyard."

"Really?" Anton asked. "How did you manage that?"

"I mentioned your beautiful eyes," Romèe said, close to Catherine's face.

Catherine waved him away, blushing at the boy's immoderate attentions. "Joan of Arc knocked on Mother's windows last night. We thought they were bats. Anton gave us candles," Catherine said, "but Mother opened the window and only lilies blew in."

"Flowers?" Romèe asked Anton. "How could that be?'

"Miracles happen," Anton said, and then led the way up the cobbled narrow street to the cathedral.

The street's forty-five degree angle was lined with tourist shops and restaurants. Racks of merchandise and eatery tables competed with jostling shoppers for available footing. All along the upward spiral of the stone avenue, Anton greeted the shop owners and restaurant managers by name.

"We are really a small village until the tourist buses arrive each day," Anton said.

Catherine jumped as Romèe pushed Anton forward. "By the time we get back down, the tours will add two hundred more people to the crunch."

"Did your father fire you then?" Anton laughed, obviously delighted to let his cousin horn in.

"For a year to tour the continent. I'm starting here." Romèe offered his hand to Catherine, who pretended to miss his intention.

"We better move, or the crowds will overtake us," she said. "We are still going to the Abbey?"

"We both know the Mont like the back of our hands," Anton said.

Romèe took her arm. "Neither of us was born on the Mont, but Anton was delivered in the hospital thirty minutes away in Avranches."

Anton chimed in, "Except for college in Caen, I've spent my life on Mont Saint Michel. I like letting the world come to my door."

Catherine noticed the cousins were the same height, both curly headed, Romèe dark, Anton the blond. "Who's the oldest?"

Romèe pointed to Anton.

"I am," Anton said, "and more responsible."

"How old are you?" Romèe asked.

"Why?" Catherine teased, pleased with all the attention.

On the way to the top, they stopped at Saint Peter's, the parish church. Inside, a silver stature of Saint Michael nearly erased the gloom and dampness of the place. Back in the sunshine outside, Catherine hugged the armored statue to the right of the entrance, which could have been St. Joan.

Hoping to re-establish her maturity in both her escorts' eyes, Catherine said, "I've decided not to go to college in Lansing, Michigan."

Anton said, "Michigan is a Native American name."

"I want to know more about Mont Saint Michel's history," Catherine said. "During the Hundred Years War the Mont remained true to France."

"Thanks to 119 defending knights," Romèe offered.

Catherine asked Anton, "Did Romèe tell you my mother is hunting the ghost of Joan of Arc here?"

"Your mother did," Anton said. "That Amazon never visited Mont Saint Michel."

Romèe said, "During wars, pilgrims headed for Saint Michel. Maybe she slipped in when the troops were stalled before Paris."

"Impossible. The countryside was ruled by the English." Anton continued the climb toward the Abbey.

"Ah, but the countrymen were French speaking," Catherine said. "Joan could have traveled at night as she did from Vaucoulers to Chinon."

Romèe seemed determined to encourage the concept. "...to bring the besieged Mont the English guns she had captured in 1429. Cardinal Louis d'Estouteville added gun turrets to the fortifications in 1421, I think it was."

Catherine added dreamily. "...to the Gabriel Tower with the two chimneys to allow the smoke from the artillery guns to escape. He was Captain of those 119 knights."

St. Joan joined the group at the mention of her name. "Just to make sure their facts are correct," she explained to Brother Richard, who reached through the thinned atmosphere and pulled himself to her side.

Brother Richard fingered the rosary beads that kept his mission with St. Joan on the right course. "Living vicariously through these young people is not the purpose you were assigned to accomplish."

"Remember when Samuel Clemens came to Mont?" St. Joan brushed between Romèe and Catherine, breaking the bond of Catherine's hand in the crook of Romèe arm.

"I admit you helped him find out his daughter died of that awful typhoid disease," Brother Richard said.

"In a sweet way." St. Joan said standing aside to allow the threesome to continue up to the Abbey.

"Yes," Brother Richard admitted somewhat reluctantly, "the dream kiss of good-bye was lovely. I am sure, when he found out that your hand brought her to him, Samuel was grateful."

"So, I have been useful?"

"I cannot out argue you," Brother Richard said, "but I know your innermost thoughts. They are not without resentments."

St. Joan backed out of reality, acknowledging her anger, "I was kicked out of my youth. An innocent, not one unwarranted deed of blemish, not one thought astray, burnt to death by truly evil people."

Anton slapped the wall of the narrowing street, "My home is a good enough rock for ghost or man, a granite jewel in a blue sea."

"Of green grass," Catherine added.

"Like your eyes," Romèe said, shamelessly flirting.

Anton stopped when they reached the foot of the Grand Staircase. "In winter the winds howl every day."

"My parents and I couldn't spend Christmas here in 1983," Romèe said. "Aunt Gail and Anton were isolated for more than a week from the mainland."

Anton looked out toward the southern coast. "You would have been two or three," Anton said to Romèe. "I was ten that year. Even at low tide, the causeway was flooded from the high seas."

Catherine quoted her guidebook, "At one time, the tides around the island were so swift the water could overtake and drown a galloping horse."

"After the retaining walls were built, the ground rose and now the sluggish syzygy tides at the spring and autumn equinox merely shift the bay silt," Anton said. "Quicksand and mud are real dangers."

"Father invested in a dredging campaign," Romèe said.

"But it failed to stop the conquering marsh grasses," Anton sighed.

Catherine spoke more to herself than to the young men. "I read a 1920 book which still showed the Couesnon River channel. They said the farmers liked the deposits of sea-sand that they used as fertilizer. The granite dust, broken shells and seaweeds teemed with iodine, phosphate and azote. In 1856 new causeways, a safety dike and the long dam of Roche

Torin were erected to steady and turn the course of the See and the Selune Rivers. Then in 1881 there was a cry against such encroachments and the ugliness of the diagonal safety dikes."

Catherine watched Romèe, as he gazed out to the shore.

"With the moon's movement away from the earth," Romèe said, "weakening the tides further, I wonder what the chances are for the vanished Scissy forest to return."

The three young people continued to climb the staircase kings and queens and entourages of lesser pilgrims had taken throughout the centuries. They followed the vaulted alleys up to the west entrance doors of the Abbey. The clouds were darkening to deeper shade of gray.

"Do I need a hat?" Catherine remembered her mother's stories about hats and gloves worn in Catholic churches.

"The rain has held off," Anton said. "Your glorious hair is crown enough for mass."

Catherine noticed Romèe's eyebrows lowered and nearly met, as he searched for something to add. "The church had to be re-consecrated after the French revolutionaries used it for a prison."

However, at the mention of her hair, Catherine slightly recalled the pink diamond from the dream when the platform had been a golden floor. Summoning the vision of the dome, Catherine stepped away from the church, into the empty courtyard. She spun in a circle, her red hair a swirl of color. "I dreamt of a butterfly filled greenhouse right here." She tried to explain to Anton, who seemed embarrassed looking around as if to see if anyone he knew had witnessed the spectacle Catherine had made of herself. "I'm afraid I'm rather infantile at times," she apologized.

Romèe stood in rapt admiration. "You are a marvelous creature. Who would want you to change?"

Catherine nodded in Anton's direction.

"Him? Father-time has him locked up." Romèe thumped Anton's shoulder. "He's afraid to enjoy anything."

"I am a post in the mud," Anton said with a short bow.

"A stick," Catherine corrected. "A stick, not a post, in the mud."

"Exactly," Romèe said, gallantly opening the church door for Catherine.

"I worry the upper doors might be locked," Anton said.

Romèe mentioned the staircases on the roof, built around 1520.

Catherine told him she wasn't suicidal. "I plan to take panoramic photographs from the bell tower, as if I stood with the original architects, beholding the view while workmen still hammered at their side. Was the Merveille finished when St. Joan was alive?"

"Another romantic," Anton said. "No, not until King Charles VII sent money after he pushed the English out of the country."

Romèe jumped, and as if the words were knocked out of him. "After Joan's trial was reversed." He looked behind himself. "Are you the culprit?" he asked Catherine. "Someone just hit me on the back."

"Imagining things," Catherine said. "The Merveille was finished before Joan of Arc was canonized in 1920."

"No, no," Romèe stammered. "That was sainthood. The Church reversed the sorcery heresy in 1454 so that Charles could be crowned by the Blessed, Venerable Joan of Arc."

"So St. Joan probably didn't see the pointed and fretted spires," Catherine felt disappointed for the Saint.

The group of three young people was lucky. No doors were locked to the cramped sets of corkscrew stairs leading up to the roof. Romèe hoisted Catherine's camera equipment up the last ladder through a trap door.

Catherine was the first to step out onto the bell-tower floor. Open arched portals surrounded them. The bells required a base platform as large as an average front room. A tired migrant dove moved an inch or two on the wide rim of an open span. Catherine readied her close-up lens and shot the blinking bird. The shutter noise spooked the small creature, who fluttered off.

Romèe touched her shoulder and asked to be shown how to snap her picture. Their hands touched as they fumbled over the mechanisms.

When she broke away from their close encounter, Catherine assumed various ridiculous stances. She laid her head on a southern ledge. With her hair hanging down the wall Romèe took her picture against the backdrop of shops and hotels far below.

"Mother will love it," Catherine said.

Then Catherine had Romèe and Anton pose. Romèe pulled Anton's cap down and then to one side.

Catherine asked Anton to take the hat off. "I like your hair mussed." Both young men messed up their own hair and then each other's. "Anton's is a golden crown even in this dull light."

Romèe said, "Everyone must tell you, you have beautiful hair."

"Red hair is a freak of nature," Catherine recited her rehearsed litany. "Less than one percent of the world's population has red hair. I might as well be an albino."

"No!" Romèe said, clearly shocked.

Anton caught the ends of Catherine's hair as she brushed it over her shoulder. As he took a step closer, Catherine held her breath. Anton raised his eyes from his hands enmeshed in her glowing hair. Catherine melted before his limpid pale eyes.

Romèe coughed loudly.

Anton asked, "May I sketch you tomorrow in the Abbey before the tourists come."

"I'll chaperone," Romèe said.

As far as Catherine was concerned Anton could have asked for her arm or for her shaven head, or her mother. "Yes," she said.

Facing Romèe's scowl, Anton quickly commented, "I sketch all my hotel guests, if they permit me to."

"Will your mother allow it?" Romèe asked, sounding like a parent.

"I'll want to sketch your mother too," Anton said, sticking out his tongue to Romèe.

Catherine composed herself by walking around the small enclosure taking pictures in every direction. She kept a view of the arches as frames for each picture. "In my dream-house I will need views in four directions. It will be a circular glass house."

"With a moving turret as its base to follow the sun's path around a mountain-rimmed lake," Romèe offered.

"Yes," Catherine said. "My mother's fiancée calls me a Chicago crocodile. I eat up everything I might use someday."

"Life is a jigsaw puzzle," Romèe said, "waiting for us to create something new and meaningful."

Anton took Catherine's hand to get her attention away from Romèe's smile. "We have to leave before the Angelus bells ring."

Catherine noticed the bird returned to its perch as they left. Rain began to fall gently.

Waiting for her mother's return from a shopping trip, Catherine sat astride her bed lotus-position-correct to observe the outer reaches of her soul. Both Catherine and her mother's room faced west. The rain had stopped for a moment and the bay's brightness touched every object in the narrow, high-ceilinged rooms. Catherine could see part of her mother's hotel room on the other side of the bright yellow bathroom. Ivy trellises held starched lace billows around the bed. The hem of the sheet and the giant pillows were embroidered with ivy. The white bed and clothes chests were stenciled with the same green pattern

Catherine had achieved a personhood separate from her mother's. Her long hair had probably caught both Romèe and Anton in its folds. Horrible to be only hair. She stuck an end of it in her mouth, trying to name the tastes. Mostly soap and perfumes, not a very substantial, long-lasting bouquet. To others her life must seem like a sip of weak wine. Neither man treated her as an appendage of her beautiful mother. To Anton she was an independent guest with enough personality as a budding architect to be preserved in some hall of remembrance. Romèe had chosen her hotel room.

A pair of parakeets in a red cage sat on the red enameled dresser. White hearts decorated all the furniture. Red cherry clusters trimmed the virgin linens of the bed and on the papered door wall pink rosebuds dangled among lace ribbons. It was a Queen-of-Heart's room. For whatever reason, Romèe seemed destined to stay in her face, stick to her like a CD's plastic wrap.

Anton's reaction to her twirling dance in front of the Abbey contrasted with Romèe's approving attention. That was the trouble. Romèe was no challenge. Anton brought out her huntress instincts. How dare he not be equally entranced as his cousin? He didn't seem shy, but then intimacy was more than idle chit-chat. If she could prove her worth to Anton, or convince him he was of interest to her as a partner, maybe Romèe could be considered equally, alongside him. As it stood, Anton was the focus of her attention.

If she cut her hair to present her soul closer to the bone than the tent of her hair allowed, would Anton be as quick to reach for his artist tools? Catherine wasn't sure her talents could be reflected in a sketch. Surely, the folds and drape of her hair created a more enticing subject. Maybe Anton should just place her wig on a post.

She loved her hair herself. Catherine could feel the constant wings of her guardian angel as they swept her shoulder with God's comfort and protection. Did Anton's dream of returning friends for life include her? Maybe she would not return. Perhaps she would never leave.

She caught her breath, as she had in the bell tower. She was falling for both of these cousins, Anton's slow blue eyes and the constant smile of Romèe. Catherine reached out both her arms toward the hotel room's door and clasped their souls before pulling her hands to her heart. They were hers. Their lives hers, her life theirs. She opened her palm and blew their souls back to them. Which one would she end up with? What would Mother say?

CHAPTER FOUR

Conversation was a series of monosyllables at Aunt Gail's evening meal. Romèe could hear the storm ranting even in the windowless dining room.

When the wine was flowing faster than the words, Aunt Gail inquired, "Had a falling out?"

"Over a girl," Romèe said.

"That redhead?" Anton sounded shocked.

"You asked to sketch her!"

Anton opened his arms wide in innocence to his mother. "But I sketch all my guests."

"You touched her hair!"

"Barely," Anton dismissed the subject, finishing his glass of wine and pouring another.

"And you stood too close," Romèe choked out in anger.

Aunt Gail was about to leave the room, but returned at this revelation. "Is she taken with Anton?"

"No," Anton said.

"Yes," Romèe said gloomily. "More than me. She called you a citizen."

"But, Romèe," Aunt Gail interrupted, "You can be a citizen."

"How?" Romèe grumbled still glaring at his cousin.

"You could buy a life-time lease on a house on the Mont," Aunt Gail said. "The Artichoke's house is free the end of August. Mr. Shaldenmere asked me if I wanted it in order to free-up the hotel for Anton."

Now Anton gave them his full attention. "What did you tell him?"

"That as soon as I was out of mourning, I would take over my sister-in-law's florist shop in Paris."

"When will that be?" Anton asked.

"We're getting side-tracked," Romèe said. "What about the house?"

"In time," Gail patted her son's hand, and then turned to Romèe. "Do you want to lease it?"

"I do, when can we?"

"I'll call the owner and have him meet us there tomorrow. Is that all right? I can lend you the down-payment for a day or two."

"Yes." Romèe even smiled at Anton. "I'll wire my father for the money as soon as I lease the house and pay you back."

Anton said. "When you chaperone the sketch tomorrow, you can tell Catherine you are a citizen."

Both young men began to devour their food.

On the third floor, Mother asked, "Sketch me, what on earth for?"

"You'd be among the guest portraits decorating the staircase, the halls and the entranceway," Catherine said. "Anton envisions the entire world coming to his doorstep. He draws migratory birds, too."

Catherine watched her mother arrange an armful of giant, blue hydrangea. Mother snipped the flower stems to create a fan of blue color against the windowpanes.

"I think he wants to see what I'll look like when I get old."

Mother glanced at the mirror checking out the newest sags and wrinkles. "Old? Older is a kinder term."

After stepping back to admire her arrangement of the flowers, Mother dumped out a group of shopping bags onto the bed. Catherine sprawled next to the bags. "Get off my earrings." Mother rolled her over and retrieved the jewelry. "How about a jaunt on the path around the island in the morning?"

Catherine's mind immediately planned photographs to capture the height of the fortress and its isolation by taking shots upward while leaving the bay's expanse in each frame. "The photos in the tourist books don't capture the excitement I feel for the Mont."

"Its historical uniqueness or the architectural challenges?" Mother asked. "In old maps three-masted ships sail in the southern bay, before the causeway existed."

"Both. How about after dinner, if the rain lets up?" Catherine lazily watched her mother put away her new clothes. "Anton said I shouldn't use fifteen rolls of film in one day. A digital would make more sense."

Mother sniffed her disapproval. "Have you explained to Anton you are an architectural student cataloging the changes of the centuries on the Mont?"

"I told Romèe too. How the builders learned by trial and error, leading to the cave-ins at the mere rumblings of thunder. Romèe listens to every word I say. I think Anton measures my words against my years. But Romèe knows I want to recreate the Mont from its first stone. I might improve the structural stability with latticed ironwork and colored glass bricks. Anton said he hoped it wouldn't change the Mont's outlines."

Mother said, "I think it would give the entire island an ethereal glow."

"Romèe agrees with you. He said the sunlight's reflection through the multi-colored panels would brighten the alleys and provide an outer radiant resonance to the whole mass."

Mother stopped hanging a new dress to say, "Romèe sounds *simpatico*."

Catherine scowled. She liked Romèe, but she wanted her mother to approve of Anton too. "Anton says I'm too young to know what I want. He feels free to be a painter, a panther, or a bore." Catherine danced over to Mother, who held onto the un-hung dress. Catherine put the dress in the closet. "Anton is 32. Romèe is only 26."

Mother banged the closet door shut. "32 is old when you're 18, but not when you are 43."

Catherine pranced around her mother in a threatening dance. "I told Romèe and Anton I create myself in front of every mirror. Anton might think he's free to walk around like a wild panther but Mother can capture anyone into tight sentences—period."

Mother laughed. "Writing Mothers can be horrid." She stopped Catherine in her tracks, playfully pushing her into a chair. "Mothers intrude their opinions into every corner of the brain. If you don't feel like talking to them, they insist on delving into the virgin territory of any emerging thought. They ruin its natural direction; diminish its originality by ascribing it to some author or politician you know you've never heard of. It can hurt."

"Romèe agrees that Joan of Arc might have made a pilgrimage to the Mont," Catherine said.

Her mother went back to straightening her new belongings. "I'm a scoundrel expert." She traversed the room arranging her jewelry in satin traveling rolls and placing scarves and lingerie in the ivy-trimmed bureau. "I married two good men and one villain; and I plan to marry the best of all when we return to the States. Without my psychic ability I could not have avoided worse dangers from thoroughly bad characters."

"I don't remember any lurking villains," Catherine said. Nevertheless, it was true her mother would be on her honeymoon with Danny when, no if, Catherine moved into the sorority.

Catherine sat very still. She remembered her own premonition dream from the night before. Running ahead of the threatening cloud of change, she had tried to warn Anton and Romèe, without realizing she was the one who needed the warning. How would she manage without Mother within an elbow's reach?

She felt her eyes dampen as she watched her beautiful mother moving away from her with each minute. Mother no longer thought of her as a daughter, just someone to spend a vacation with before abandoning her. Catherine rubbed her palms on the arms of the chair. Couldn't she have waited to remarry? Of course not. That would be silly. Why would Mother want to suffer loneliness just so her daughter could bring home dirty laundry and gossip?

Catherine was not disturbed by her mother's ability to renew passion for the opposite sex. Not that Catherine didn't miss poor Jimmy, or her own father, Simon Kerner. Jimmy's trust lawyer, the new Danny Passantino, naturally had won her mother over. They knew everything about each other, knew each owned integrity. Danny's fortune made Jimmy's comfortable legacy a mere pittance in the scheme of things; but to understand Mother's motivation to marry Danny Passantino, people needed to hear her describe how Italian men move in their suits. Mother meant she could imagine Danny's perfect body approaching without clothes. They had met for the first time at Jimmy's funeral.

The loneliness had to be faced. She looked around the room, even the furniture seemed distant. The end table next to her chair held an ornate pewter pitcher. The backdrop of the blue hydrangea enhanced its beauty.

As her mother puttered about, she didn't appear to be a crusty old broad. Instead, she had a softness, which couldn't be linked to coyness or syrupiness. Her storehouse of marvel translated the world into something possibly worthwhile.

Catherine's attention fixated on the pewter vase trying to pinpoint a vague uneasiness caused by a new tone in her mother's voice. The vase's handle seemed unlikely to provide a sure grip. The pitcher perched unsteadily on a small table next to the armchair. The wide lip of its spout offset the weight of an unsymmetrical base and rounded feet.

"Mother, you don't like Anton," Catherine said.

Mother backed into the small table and sure enough, the pewter pitcher tipped and tumbled to the floor. Mother laughed nervously, "You've spilled the beans."

Catherine helped her mother retrieve the marbles and coins stored in it.

Mother said, "Don't interpret good manners for his hotel guests as affectionate acts. Be careful of your feelings tomorrow morning, when Anton sketches you."

Catherine didn't have the heart to inform her mother she had decided to capture either Anton or Romèe in order to stay on the Mont.

At eight o'clock, they chose a cave resembling restaurant on the hotel's side of the curving walkway to the Abbey for dinner. Candles were lit to enhance the electricity, but gloom held sway. The yellow shadows outlined each fold of the tablecloths. The mirrors and shelves of wine display reflected the eerie atmosphere. Catherine expected the spaghetti sauce to appear brown instead of bright red. She ate in silence as her mother recited the plans that Danny and she had made for their coming years together. Catherine matched each dream with one of her own for Romèe or Anton.

Mother's life seemed ten times as real as Catherine's imaginary future. Not once was Catherine tempted to share her fledgling plans for staying on the Mont. Instead, she held forth about the possibility of St. Joan walking the path they had tread to the restaurant. "I think the people believed Merlin's prophecy that Joan of Arc was the virgin that would save France."

Mother held a fork filled with a bite of lamb, hesitating to speak before she placed it in her mouth. "Well, the poor child did die a virgin."

"I hope to give mine up shortly," Catherine said. "Do you remember your first time?"

"Absolutely." Mother smiled from the taste of lamb or the initial sexual experience.

"Were you married?"

"No," Mother said, "but your father and I were engaged. The cake was even ordered." Mother stopped as if to consider her daughter's options. "I'm glad you will have a career under your belt before you marry."

Catherine busied herself with putting more oil on a bite of bread. "You didn't."

"I've never worked; except to write, it's true. I did get a degree, finally. But nowadays the world presents plenty of opportunities for young women."

"Marrying not to be lonely is one of them," Catherine looked directly into her mother's face.

"Heavens, Catherine, concentrate on the Mont. You're not going to be here forever."

"You're leaving too," Catherine snapped.

Mother finished her entire meal before saying, "We will miss each other. But school will fill your days."

Catherine bent down placing her napkin next to her plate to hide her tears. "The Mont is a beautiful place. I'm glad we came. I wish I could stay longer."

"You can always come back," Mother said. "I've visited the Grand Canyon and Niagara Falls more than once."

"Yes," Catherine felt spiteful, "each time you married."

"You are that afraid to be alone?"

"No." Catherine insisted, but didn't believe her own denial.

"I'm healthier with a partner," Mother said, "saner, too."

"Can you imagine Joan of Arc married?" Catherine asked to change the subject, slightly.

"After her mission was accomplished?".

"No, before," Catherine said. "I wonder if she filled all that quiet on the hill top in France with her Voices."

Mother hugged her shoulder. "She was a lot younger than you. All the instructions from her Voices made sense. Without the sanction of Saints, neither she nor her people would have believed the aspiring miracle of taking France back from the English."

"But how did the idea come upon her, specifically?"

Mother motioned for the waiter and asked for a dessert menu. Then she said, "St. Joan was fourteen when her village was overrun and the cattle taken. Her natural vigor and the scope of her mind must have demanded remedy."

"Domremy. She was in love with religion," Catherine mused. "When Saint Michael spoke, she didn't know it was heresy to believe him."

"But she kept her mission a secret for four years," Mother said. "Do you want the cherry or chocolate custard?"

"You take the chocolate and I'll take the cherry," Catherine knew they would share each dish. "Robert de Baudricourt," she said. "I never believed the miracle eggs laid for him by Mark Twain."

"Joan was a sane and shrewd girl, according to Bernard Shaw. She did know about the Herring Battle, and might have predicted its outcome by listening to peasant friends before the magistrate heard the news through official sources. I think St. Joan convinced the six knights to go with her to the king before she presented Baudricourt her demands for an escort."

Catherine compared her intrigues to nail down Anton or Romèe before approaching her mother about not returning to the States. "That was quite a feat," Catherine said.

"And she was just warming up," Mother said.

Her mother apologized for chewing her ear off about her wedding plans. When they had finished the ices, Mother left a huge tip for the waiter, as if paying rent for the table itself.

St. Joan and Brother Richard watched Catherine and her mother head back to Hotel de Bermont.

"Those eggs always worried me," St. Joan said. "They were not miraculous."

Brother Richard comforted her. "In a way they were. They proved all the people were behind your heavenly mission, even if the powers in charge could not see the truth."

"But wasn't it a sin to hide the eggs and to lie to Robert?"

"Surely," Brother Richard reached for his beads, as he was wont to do whenever discussing the finer points of belief with St. Joan. "But the greater good prospered in spite of the real sin, God forgave their simple chicanery."

CHAPTER FIVE

Monday morning, Romèe waited for Anton and Aunt Gail to come down for breakfast. Unable to sleep in, he had set the dining room table with a yellow tablecloth and napkins, silverware, white plates and knobby white glasses. The name of the china, milk glass, sprung unbidden from his memory. He poured the juice and made coffee; but after all the years spent on the Mont, Romèe did not feel comfortable enough in his aunt's kitchen to rummage around for eggs or toast.

He was surprised by his own excitement. Owning a house, or even the lease on a house, was a milestone in his life. The first step in his plans to begin a career on Mont Saint Michel and to ask Catherine to start a married life with him required a secure place on the island. Romèe waltzed around the table surveying his handiwork. He wasn't sure he liked the maroon color of the walls or the rug's pattern.

Would she want lighter or at least brighter paint, maybe light blue walls and pale wood floors? The room would need more than the crystal vase of yellow tulips on the heavy-legged table to change its Moorish look. Perhaps a mirrored wall covered by a white wooden lattice with a frame of faux fig trees could modernize the ancient room.

Thinking of Catherine caused Romèe to sigh just as Aunt Gail arrived from the parlor and Anton entered from the kitchen. They laughed at him.

"Lovesick," Anton diagnosed.

"Hungry?" Aunt Gail asked.

"I didn't want to make any noise," Romèe strove for a dignified tone, "or I would have made my father's English scrambled eggs."

"Come along," Aunt Gail said. "We can talk while you show us my brother's secret egg recipe."

"What kind of a kitchen does the Artichoke house have?" Romèe asked.

"It's small, a Pullman kitchen, you Americans call it," Aunt Gail said. "Compact enough for a train car, I guess."

"Do all women want huge kitchens?" Romèe stirred the eggs and butter as he lifted the frying pan from the burner to control the heat. Pan in hand, he turned around to survey his aunt's restaurant-size kitchen.

"My husband's family fed their guests," Aunt Gail explained the mammoth proportions of the room. "Maybe Shelby will want to put in a breakfast nook or a family room with a television."

"We would need a satellite dish," Anton said. "And besides, I like it the way it is. Where can you find a stove like this to let soup simmer all day?"

"Who would want to?" Aunt Gail asked. "I find cooking repetitive and boring."

"I find it restful," Anton said. "Maybe I'll cook after I'm married."

"What if Catherine, I mean Shelby, wants to redecorate?" Romèe asked, minding his eggs.

"We'll let her," Aunt Gail said. "I was afraid to hurt my husband's feelings or I would have thrown out half the junk. Have you looked in the attic lately? I didn't unpack most of my wedding presents. There was no room to put them. I guess I can take them with me to set up a house in Paris."

"Is the Artichoke house furnished?" Romèe led the food parade back to the dining room.

"Empty even of draperies and carpets." Aunt Gail said. "Mr. Shaldenmere says tenants like to create their own worlds."

"Shelby says a home is the outer extension of the soul," Anton said, and then coughed as they focused their attention on him.

In the dining room, Romèe placed his napkin in his lap and concentrated on eating slowly, politely. He buttered only a bit of his toasted croissant, laying his knife at the top of his plate. After two bites of the buttered, fluffy scrambled eggs, he forced himself to place his fork in his plate. He sipped his orange juice and sighed.

Anton and Aunt Gail seemed to be eating in slow motion.

"Don't you like the eggs?" Romèe asked finally.

"You know they're delicious," Aunt Gail said.

"I think he's anxious to sign his first lease." Anton swallowed the last bite on his plate.

"Do you realize," Aunt Gail asked, "Romèe, just how far out on a limb you are, about Catherine's return of your affection?"

Romèe had to admit he was in a rush. He laughed. "I'm out here on my favorite tree branch sawing away."

Anton checked his watch, "Today's the day I promised to sketch Catherine."

Romèe gulped. He had forgotten, too. "I need to chaperon you."

"How can you be in two places at once?" Aunt Gail asked.

That morning before the sun was up, Catherine tried on outfits for the sketching session with Anton. In her white chemise, she carefully held a long blue dress over her head letting it slip down her arms. She crowned her hair with a floppy-brimmed hat. Waltzing around the room, Catherine returned to glimpse her prim mask in front of the pedestal mirror. Catherine threw the hat across the room and yanked the dress and the chemise off.

She looked better without clothes. Maybe Anton intended a nude sketch. Catherine stood closer to the oval mirror. Her breasts could not be any bigger or they would start to droop, but her waist could be tighter against her backbone.

She pulled the vanity stool over to the mirror. The only thing to do was to bring her knee up to hide the slight roundness of her stomach. If she hugged her pink knee just right, her arms pushed her breasts together and the nipples pointed straight ahead. She would need something to rest her foot on to pose for Anton.

Catherine started to re-dress. She thought about a seduction scene in an old movie where the actress undressed for her lover. Simplicity was definitely called for if she planned to keep eye contact with Anton while she disrobed. Red shorts and a tight tea-shirt would not delay Anton's artistic endeavors.

Catherine practiced her innocent smile for the mirror's reflection.

St. Joan and Brother Richard looked at each other on the far side of the mirror's world.

"Young girls rehearse, I guess," Brother Richard said.

"Good thing you are under angelic disguise, Brother," St. Joan teased.

"Beauty is always a delight," Brother Richard defended himself. "Does Romèe know Catherine's plans for Anton?"

In a somewhat piqued tone, St. Joan answered, "How should I know?" Then she immediately felt badly for her shortness. "Was my innocence displayed at such a rakish angle?"

Brother Richard switched off the mirror's image and faced his favorite saint. "You were a true martyr, virginal in thought, courageous in every deed."

"Save one." St. Joan hung her head. "Do you think that's why were still out here, on the edges of Heaven?"

"You recanted with good reason and withdrew the paucity of truth at your first opportunity." Brother Richard felt his loyalty deepen. "I suppose we are linked because I wanted to be at your side from the first moment I heard your fame in France."

St. Joan laughed. "So you wanted to be famous, too?"

"I did," Brother Richard admitted. "I only succeeded in being mentioned in your trial as a charlatan, a reprobate."

St. Joan tried to calm her purgatoried friend. "I only told them what I had spoken to King Charles about you."

"That my mission was folly," Brother Richard tried to control a tremor in his voice.

"Well, we are past that now, aren't we?" St. Joan watched her arm disappear around Brother Richard's fading image.

Romèe, Anton, and Aunt Gail met Catherine in the small lobby of the Hotel de Bermont.

"Am I late?" Catherine asked.

"Not at all," Romèe said. "I have to renege. I have an appointment with Aunt Gail and cannot chaperone you. Is your mother awake?"

"We needn't bother her." Catherine headed the party out into the street.

"Then, I will join you shortly," Romèe called as he and Aunt Gail headed down the hill.

"Do you need a chaperone," Catherine teased Anton.

"I think I'm safe," Anton grinned.

The smile undermined his safe position in Catherine's plans. As far as she was concerned, it was open season on all the males on the Mont.

In the Chapel of Saint Etienne, Anton placed a campstool for Catherine under the arch of a stoned-up, mold-encrusted fireplace. He sat opposite on the top step of an exit with his back against a locked, black iron gate. The scant sea light danced behind him.

Catherine perched contentedly under the arch. The anteroom was a bit chilly for shorts and she could smell something old and unclean in the Abbey's air moving down the steps past them toward the exit. She asked Anton what to do while he was sketching.

"Think pleasant thoughts," he said.

For Catherine, to breathe was to talk. "One of my new guide books says this was the ossuary, where the bones were kept, but my 1927 book says they are stacked in the chapel for cripples behind Saint Peter's that leads to the citizens' cemetery."

Anton admonished her, "Don't babble."

Babble? How long she had been talking? When he touched the box of charcoals, she remembered saying she hadn't brought any to Mont Saint Michel. "The camera seemed sufficient, but now I want my hand on more creative supplies." The camera felt like a pen that didn't write. "May I borrow more of yours?" Then she had carried on about her plans, not saying she secretly hoped he would save her from school. "Living alone for the first time, I'm going to eat ice cream and cake for breakfast. Mother's wedding is to be staged as soon as we return to America." Catherine ran down the list of Mother's marriages and what she had thought of the short-lived men. "You'd be surprised how little I recall about Daddy." She had articulated quite clearly about their old house in Ann Arbor including Mother's decorating errors with primary colors and her mother's genetic lack of a crucial female attribute; i.e., cooking. She'd added to keep him up-to-date, "Mother's new fiancé comes equipped with a Jamaican cook."

Anton only grumbled behind his sketch.

"Men find it hard to switch subjects," Catherine said. "Something about less connections between the different halves of their brains. That's why you can concentrate for longer periods of time. Men actually accomplish a lot of isolated achievements without regard for how they change the world's environment, or people's lives. Only a woman's brain remembers the laundry needs to be taken out of the dryer, while the cake requires only ten more minutes to be tested with a toothpick, and some child expects to be picked up from a soccer game in twenty minutes at the same time that she puts finishing touches on a Christmas tree or hairdo."

Anton only sighed.

Catherine continued, "Contrariwise a man requires assistance to move from one subject of conversation to the next. You all are incapable of seeing connections between the story of a shopping trip for couches and the listing of family heirlooms to be handed down to my eight children when I get around to accepting a husband, losing my virginity and finishing my architectural degree." Poor guy. Catherine could see his mind was locked on the pencil point as he drew her outline. Babble indeed.

He was just incapable of listening while his eyes and hand were busy. He wasn't even chewing the gum she'd given him. Anton was probably a step ahead of most men, able to use *two* of his faculties at the same time.

Catherine grinned and Anton moaned as the line of her lips shifted again, even without talking.

He was right, she could *not* stop talking and listened to her voice describing, "My first view of Mont Saint Michel was in the travel section of my home-town paper." Her voice was high-pitched from nervousness and seemed to bounce off the slate floor. "I thought Walt Disney patterned Fantasy Land after it; but that was a castle in Germany."

Catherine did not like Anton's transition from a supplicating porter and guide to a demanding artist. She wondered how his other guests had viewed the leap from amanuenses to dictator. It made her pout.

"Stop that!" Anton yelled.

Catherine set her mouth in a placid half grin, thinking men made her gums ache. Her throat was dry from all the talking and she felt her anger bringing a hot-pink blush up from the base of her ears.

Anton gave up. "The light has moved." Catherine helped him pick up the sketching tools. Anton said, "I know the perfect place behind the altar where the light falls from three windows."

They hurried through the gloomy three-tiered Romanesque nave, marched through the centuries' shadow hues into the airy Gothic choir where steps led up to the deserted altar stone.

Anton arranged his tools. "May I sketch you nude?" He pulled out a green towel from his drawing satchel and placed it close to the altar. As if she had been modeling for years, Catherine stepped out of her shorts, pulled her top off and tried to pose gracefully. Anton arranged her hair to catch the light streaming from the stained-glass windows.

Catherine directed him to, "Angle the mirror so I can see your sketch pad."

She watched him block out his pad and then start to draw her hips with short pencil strokes. As she noticed him line her thigh, she reached to scratch her knee.

"You can't move!" Anton shouted.

But Catherine's flesh moved under his pencil. His hands seemed to bring warmth to her ankles, calves, and belly. Her fingers relaxed as Anton drew up her arms, along her rib cage and down her shoulders.

As he outlined the shape of her breasts and nipples, Catherine's fingers twitched. She tried to concentrate on listening to her own silence, not unlike the pink sea shell casing sound she'd held to her ear as a child. Hearing pink now she thought of the great dim sausages of stone pillars closely packed in the underpinnings of the cathedral. Pink underthings of garments and flesh contained a quiet here-now sound more akin to reality than the white noise of freeway traffic or restaurant chatter.

Catherine's ears became sensitive to these structural harmonics while she sat devoid of trappings. Having reached their pinnacle of growth, her bones cried out to be remembered in their shy casing of skin. Surely, courage was first born in pink sounds. Newborns must hear initial applause while struggling into the rosy world.

When Catherine saw Anton draw her facial features in the angled mirror, she felt another hot blush rising to her hairline and when his pencil touched her lips, she sighed and their eyes met.

"I'm...I'm almost done," Anton said.

Catherine heard a slight step accompanied by cloth snuffling sounds. A solid advance of step upon step approached down the cathedral's side aisle with a definite swirling of broad cloth between stiff legs. Catherine tried to hear pink petticoats with ruffled lace but the coarse noise was not silk. She opened her eyes to find a priest taking a good look at Anton's sketch in the mirror's reflection.

"What are you two doing back there?" he asked.

Anton stood up and flipped the sketchbook cover over his drawing.

Catherine slipped on her top and shorts. "It's an art class." Catherine watched the priest fidget with his belt. She smiled to think she was undressing him in her mind, probing the black-buttoned cassock to let her fingers find any pink in his nervous parts. As Catherine let her imagination grope along the priest's leg, she wondered if parts could atrophy from lack of use.

But the priest knew Anton and gave him what for, adding, "The tour group might have caught you!"

Anton apologized as he introduced Father Damion to Catherine.

A moment later, the door of the church swung open to let in the day's first group of tourists. Light flooded the long aisle of escape from the priest's censure. Catherine carried Anton's open box of charcoal and pencils. Anton motioned for her to sit down next to him under the fortified arch of Claudine Towers. As Catherine hurried to his side, the box tipped and colored pencils rolled down the steps with the charcoal pieces bouncing after them.

CHAPTER SIX

Halfway down the stairs, Romèe caught the fleeing art tools. "I've got them," he sang up to Catherine and Anton, scooping up the scramble of pencils as they rolled slowly down several steps to him.

"Romèe saves the day." Still perched on the stone bench, Anton laughed.

Bright with embarrassment, Catherine laid the empty box down next to Anton.

"The priest interrupted Anton's sketch," she told Romèe as they replaced the fallen supplies. "He's a weird guy."

"Father Damion," Anton explained for Romèe.

"Aunt Gail sets her clocks by him," Romèe said.

"My mother won't return to the Catholic church until the Pope has a reason to wear a dress," Catherine said. Anton ignored her. "Did you hear me? You know, like when the Pope is a woman."

Anton nodded his head.

But Romèe said, "In Tahiti, the altars were used for the Holy of Holies. When a virginal man and virginal woman created life, the tribe stood around the altar shouting instructions and encouragements." Then, Romèe puffed out his chest and stood with his feet wide apart as if his next words needed a sturdy stance, "You are now looking at a life-time citizen of the Mont."

"I've already found one," Catherine said, sidling up to place her bare thigh next to Anton's tight jeans. Anton did not move. "Do you want to finish the sketch?"

Anton said, "I...I have to sketch your mother."

Catherine stepped away from Anton.

Romèe' felt his brows lower and his chest deflated. He chatted on about trivialities, offering to buy them a cup of coffee in the shop at the bottom of the Grand Staircase. "Before we attempt maneuvering through the crowds back down to the hotel."

"Did you lease the house then?" Anton asked Romèe.

"Mr. Shaldenmere was late for his appointment, so I left to catch you two," Romèe said. "He's quite fond of Aunt Gail."

In the restaurant Catherine stirred cream into her cup of coffee, but it turned a sullen gray instead of an appetizing tan. Neither Anton nor Romèe seemed to notice the awful stuff. She half expected the coffee brew to dissolve the plastic spoon and did not attempt to sip the gray sludge. Was Anton's sketching seduction real?

'Believe what they tell you,' Mother's words filtered through her pain. He had to sketch Mother, that was all. Anton's interest in her would rekindle itself. "Go ahead," she said, dismissing them. "I want to watch the tourists."

Anton patted her back as he left them.

Romèe said, "They are as regular as the tide of pilgrims who came before the French Revolution."

Catherine went out of the restaurant to sit on a sunny stone baluster. Romèe joined her without questioning the move. Catherine's back was warmed by the next step's collection of heat.

"A stone throne," Romèe said.

Catherine rubbed her throat to stop the ache left from not allowing herself to weep. Apparently, she was not sufficient onto herself. She could not point to any accomplishment or bevy of friends. Mother was a comfort she would have to learn to live without, so Anton's coldness hurt.

Romèe must have noticed she was upset. "Do you want to talk about it?"

She shook her head wishing he would disappear. No matter how she turned it over, Anton was more interested in his pursuits, the offhand conquest of her nudity for his sketchbook and the priest's good opinion, than of her. "Anton doesn't care to search out my soul while he sketches my toes, fingernails...," Catherine added in a whisper, "...and pubic hairs."

Romèe stood, slamming his fist into the rock wall.

Catherine felt a cottony taste on the back of her throat, the dusty dryness of fear. "What if the world is always this disinterested in me?" she asked Romèe. "Using me without a second thought?"

Romèe sat down next to her, sucking on his injured knuckles. "I'm interested. My stupid cousin...."

Catherine brushed her fingertip over her top lip and stuck her tongue out to taste it. A slight tang of orange lingered on the skin. As her saliva glands reacted, her tongue unglued itself from the roof of her mouth and her fear of the world's coldness lessened. "Okay," she said, uncrossing her legs from their cramped position, "I'll just have to conquer you all. You can't kill me."

Romèe smiled. "We would have to use a gun or a blunt instrument. No one can scare you to death."

"Joan of Arc had to face her fears alone."

"Course, she had more than rejection to worry about."

"She had the English running through her village pillaging the cattle and gardens." Catherine could finally smile. "St. Joan called them 'god-damns' because they swore so much."

"But there must have been an hour when her terrors clutched her throat and her voices didn't fill the void of loneliness," Romèe said.

"Maybe after she recanted."

"She's telling the story half right," St. Joan commented to Brother Richard as they peeked over the wall where the couple was resting.

"The fears came before you recanted," Brother Richard said.

"The perceived fire seemed more real than their actually torching of me."

"The Lord understood they were torturing your mind to distraction." Brother Richard offered St. Joan a clean cloth for her tears. "All the talk of damning your soul for not receiving communion, while at the same time they were insisting you wear a dress to attend mass."

"The thoughts of the fire singeing me brought me close to losing my soul. But the air left my lungs in the surge of upward heat and my spirit floated in horror above my smoking carcass. I was saved from the worst of the pain by my Lord."

"You did redeem yourself," Brother Richard said.

"Yes, in the end I assured them I was sent by God. Wasn't that an odd thing," She looked Brother Richard straight into his spirit face, "to claim so assuredly that God had sent me to save France?"

"The assuredness was the strangest," Brother Richard agreed. "Many of us have thought, in error, that we received messages from God."

"But everyone around me believed," St. Joan said. "France needed saving and they listened to my plans."

"As if you were sent by God?" Brother Richard realized her actual question.

St. Joan's tone softened. "How brave I was to believe with them."

Brother Richard tried to boost her spirits. "France would only be an old word, if you had not rescued us from the English."

"The Lord could have stopped me."

"He could have changed the tenor of the messages you were receiving," Brother Richard said, "but He let you save France."

Catherine continued to chat with Romèe, "I need to knit together a golden armor of defenses. The links will be my future unadorned by male consorts."

"But..." Romèe said.

"Buildings of my design could be comfort enough." As Catherine stood up her knees seemed to reverberate with the humiliation of Anton's rejection. "Anton got me down to my roots,' she said, sitting down stiffly.

Romèe rubbed the sides of her knees before letting her attempt the downhill trek to the hotel. His hands were warm, the result healing, as if her mother or a sudden brother had touched her sympathetically.

They had to push their way through the onslaught of upward-bound tourists and pilgrims.

"You can tell who has given up in the crowd," Romèe said. "No attempt at recognition stirs their brains. Their eyes don't match faces to those in their memories."

Catherine felt a shudder from the moving zombies as she hunted for warmth from hopeful people in the crowd. "There's a live one."

A woman older than Catherine's mother, dressed in soft blues with bright mischievous eyes passed them.

"There's another," Romèe said, nodding toward a fat girl probably five years younger than Catherine, dressed in huge red-and-white polka dots, and laughing at an equally fat friend's remark.

Romèe and Catherine nodded in agreement at a child in a stroller and a dark old man with a peaceful, courteous manner.

Some tourists lived. Two out of ten seemed able to handle the discouragement life promised. The zombies walked in a daze able to see non-human beings. Dogs and cats and flowers lit their low-banked fires. Otherwise, the disembodied souls bumped into each other, while carefully avoiding tables or trash cans.

"I half expect them to say excuse me to the tables," Catherine said.

"People have stopped existing for them."

Catherine determined to keep her eyes open to find someone who needed others. "I imagine on some verandah in my future, maybe in Hawaii where bugs will be swept away in the trade winds, a pool of my friends will assemble to contemplate ideal communities under the moon's growing population. But none of my friends are here."

As they reached the open doorway to the hotel, Catherine stopped. "But like, where are my mother's friends? Husbands sure, but do you have to marry a friend to keep them?"

"Friends are like well-kept secrets," Romèe said, taking her hand. "You have to be as ready for friends as if you were catching butterflies, alert, with a sticky unseen net or two, like me."

Catherine pulled away, still smarting from Anton's coldness. "Or let them fly away to other attractions."

"Find contentment in the search."

Did she see a tear glistening in his long lashes? "Like Jimmy with his fishing line in some fishless stream?"

"Your mother's late husband?"

"All late," Catherine said, despondently.

Romèe touched her shoulder lightly, "You have me, forever."

The genteel quiet of the Bermont upstairs parlor vanished. Romèe slammed into the room. "What! Am I invisible?"

Aunt Gail wiped up the sudden spill of tea in her flowered saucer with her napkin. "You appear quite angry. Does that help?"

Romèe slumped in a chair, but was able to intake the offered nourishment of pecan rolls and tea. "Catherine. It's Catherine," he said between swallows. He balanced his third hot cup quite deftly as he marched around the room, muttering to himself. "And your son!"

The accompanying angry sweep of his arm rocked the lamp next to Aunt Gail's chair, but she continued to sip her tea. "Anton is involved?"

"Sketching," Romèe stomped implying the problem, then added because his aunt failed to fathom the significance of the statement, "nude. He seduced her!"

Luckily Aunt Gail's cup rested on the tea table. She clapped her hands once, loudly. "Never. He loves...."

Chastised, Romèe calmed down. "Sorry, Aunt Gail. I didn't mean he laid a hand on her."

Anton had the bad luck to enter the room. "We are out of bread, again. These Americans eat more bread...." Both Aunt Gail and Romèe stared at him. "What?" Anton asked, palms up in a plea of innocence.

"Catherine posed for you?"

"Yes, yes." Anton impatiently accepted a cup of tea.

"She's falling in love," Romèe said.

"With you?" Anton smiled sweetly as his mother offered cake.

Romèe lunged toward Anton's chair before regaining his composure. "With you, you idiot." Romèe fell back into his chair. "She can't even see me, or hear me."

Anton looked for help from his mother. "I've done nothing wrong."

"Apparently, Catherine's feelings are heading in your direction," Aunt Gail straightened the tea table.

"When I told her, *I* was a life-time citizen," Romèe grumbled, "she said she already *had* one."

"No idea," Anton shook his head.

"Oh," Romèe spread his arms to mock Anton's previous displays of innocence. "Asking a young girl to take off her clothes is innocent nowadays."

"I misjudged her maturity," Anton agreed. "Shelby will understand."

"Romèe," Aunt Gail spoke softly as if to quell the escalating battle. "If Catherine doesn't return your affection...."

"She will," Romèe said with more confidence than he felt. "She'll love me because I love her entirely."

"What do you see in the scamp?" Anton taunted. He scooted his chair back as Romèe made a move toward him.

"See?" Romèe was close to tears of rage. "I know her heart. She's ready to love, she loves Mont Saint Michel the way I do."

Anton shook his head. "You'll both get island fever the way I do."

"I want to be Prometheus Bound to Catherine," Romèe said. "She's a talented architect without being trained. She needs me. I love her down to her toenails. And her eyes...." Romèe lapsed into silence, awed by his vision of Catherine.

"But even if she eventually accepts you," Aunt Gail said. "Your father is counting on you."

"Father loves me," Romèe explained. "My degree in business can help a lot of companies. I could open a branch of Mother's florist business here. Now that it will be your business, you know I'll be a reliable asset for you here."

"True," Aunt Gail said. "And the island needs a flower outlet."

Romèe sat down in the too-soft chair next to the bay window. "But I still have to kill off your only son."

They laughed together in relief.

"What do you want me to do?" Anton asked them.

"Explain you're engaged," Romèe and Aunt Gail said in unison.

"I will when no one is around to embarrass the poor girl. I've already set up a meeting with her in the cellar of the Merveille, tomorrow at four." Anton sulked out of the room.

"Follow me," Aunt Gail said to Romèe. He did, through the back door of the kitchen up the back staircase to the roof. If only he could think of a way to lock-in Catherine's attention, as Anton had. "Hurry along," Gail motioned for him from his uncle's greenhouse.

"I didn't think you used this anymore."

"Anton wants a hot tub in here," Gail said. "I keep putting him off because I have a surprise for him. He thinks I'm come up here to mourn his father, but I don't very much anymore." She stepped away from the door so Romèe could enter.

At first he thought the figure to be a person. The small mannequin wore a white wedding dress.

"It's time for Shelby to come home," Gail said with a triumphant smile. "And I have to start packing."

"She'll love the gown." Romèe knew he should comment on the intricacies of the dress but they were beyond his vocabulary. "But why do you have to leave?"

"You see the trouble Anton is getting into without trying. Shelby will set him straight. And, they need their own home."

"I'll miss you," he managed.

Shelby had finished college while boarding at the convent in Paris. It made sense for the wedding to happen now. Romèe gave his aunt the credit for all the good planning. Shelby had survived her drunken step-father's sexual advances by jumping ship in the English Channel and swimming into the bay. Only twelve at the time and fearful of being returned to the man, Shelby refused to give her real name. Aunt Gail had swept her up into her life, like the daughter she had always dreamt of having. One year later, Aunt Gail discovered Anton kissing Shelby in the kitchen and she whisked the girl off to the Paris convent for schooling and safety.

Romèe thought the four years of mourning rather conveniently meshed with the remaining years necessary for Shelby's college degree. Anton never seemed to question his mother. Perhaps he wanted to prove his worthiness to both Shelby and his mother.

The wedding dress stood as a mute testimony to a mother's love for her son and her new daughter-in-law.

Romèe asked. "Will you send Anton to bring her home now?"

"He's scheduled for a visit to the convent. I'll tell him to set the date." Aunt Gail pulled the braid of her hair over her shoulder, twisting the ties tighter. "Shelby will need new clothes, I'm sure."

"There's a lot to arrange."

"Oh, I meant to tell you at tea, Mr. Shaldenmere phoned his apologies. We'll try again tomorrow." Aunt Gail ushered him out of the greenhouse. "Don't tell Anton about the dress, yet. If you go with him tomorrow, you could see your mother for the lease loan."

"I will," Romèe said. "But Anton is supposed to sketch Catherine's mother and didn't he have an appointment at four with Catherine?"

"I'll explain to Catherine and invite her mother to dinner. Might as well get to know them better, now that you intend to make them part of the family."

Romèe roughly bear-hugged his aunt. "Thanks for believing I can make Catherine happy."

"Oh, that," his aunt smiled. "When Anton returns, I'll join you in Paris for a shopping trip with Shelby. Maybe Mrs. Marksteiner will come with me."

"To leave Catherine and Anton alone?"

"He'll have enough time to explain without embarrassing her in front of us. I'm sure he'll put in a good word for you."

CHAPTER SEVEN

Catherine idly paged through the Dome of St. Joan sketchbook. She would have the rest of her life to rue the interrupted opportunity to nail Anton's hide to hers. Priests were un-necessary evils in the world, she supposed.

"Keeping out of mischief?" Mother asked.

"Not if I can help it."

"When did you complete these?" Mother sounded impressed.

"I think I was half-asleep. My hand seems to know them, but see how faint the lines are? I hardly remember drawing them."

"I would take another nap, if I were you." Mother placed a pencil in Catherine's hand.

Suddenly Catherine felt very tired. Tired of Mother, Romèe, architecture and even the quest for Anton.

Her mother noticed the lethargy. "All those raging hormones are bound to tire you out periodically. I'll go down and ask Anton for a larger sketch pad."

"And food." Catherine mumbled a good-bye or thanks before her body demanded repair.

Whenever Catherine or Romèe conjured the ghost of Joan of Arc by mentioning her name on Mont Saint Michel, St. Joan wished she could answer all their questions about her stay on the Mont. "I knew I was in great peril when I failed to convince King Charles to follow up his coronation with a sweep of Paris."

St. Joan moved the sleeping Catherine's arm to retrace the first, fading traces of the Dome.

Brother Richard stood idly by, a witness to the haunting. "Contemplating flight to Scotland was what the dauphin had envisioned for himself before your initial visit."

"My Voices were silent. They didn't mention securing Mont Saint Michel with English guns, but I knew the Mont was supplied by Scottish blockade runners. They could have taken me to a safe exile in Scotland."

St. Joan turned a page in the sketchbook to portray a side view of her Dome.

"I wish being dead meant I never had to hear people defame me."

"That Englishman, Shakespeare, lost a bit of his glory in my book," Brother Richard said.

St. Joan laughed. "Vitriolic name calling: 'Drab from the ditches of Lorraine,' 'devil's milkmaid' 'and 'Armagnas whore,' hardly endeared him to me, either."

Brother Richard tried to comfort his charge, "Nevertheless, those old religious judges paid in the afterlife for calling you a trumpery imp."

"At the time of the trial, my voices reminded me of my love for a good fracas. 'Answer boldly and God will sustain you.'"

Lacking similar means of communication with the living while in the hereafter realms assigned to her, St. Joan had to make do with implanting ideas into the heads of her chosen.

Peeking through the hotel's mullioned windows, hidden in the shadows of the Mont, St. Joan was not content to merely endow Catherine with courage. St. Joan's plans included the mate chosen for Catherine, the florist with her mother's name, Romèe. Romèe's family finances and influence were necessary to fund the design approval and construction of the pink crystal Dome of St. Joan.

As Catherine nodded in her sleep, her haunted hand reworked the drawings. St. Joan hovered near her, wondering at the passive mass of curdling glands and restless nerves in her prone protégée. Reaching out a tender index finger, the saint touched the middle of Catherine's forehead right above the bridge of the nose. The pituitary gland sent shivers of anticipation up St. Joan's arm. The drive to mate with the other half of creation rocked the remnants of bones in St. Joan.

Detaching from the motionless shell of Catherine, St. Joan rested against the bedstead. "Is this what my father assumed I felt for the neighborhood boy he picked out for me?"

"What was his name?" Brother Richard asked.

St. Joan laughed. "I never deemed the sound of his name worthy of a moment's thought. All my energy was focused on the English. How to push them out of France." St. Joan laughed again. "Remember the letter I dictated to them, "'I came here to smite you body to body, out of the realm of France'."

"Your affections were fixed in zealous pursuit of your visions."

"Saint Michael was the most awesome," St. Joan said. "His splendiferous, heavenly grandeur out-shone Saint Catherine and Saint Margaret."

St. Joan tried singing to Catherine in the tune of the old Chanson of Roland, "I came here to inspire you, stone by stone, to build the Dome of St. Joan."

St. Joan considered perhaps a short-circuit let the energy of youth drain away into the useless pursuit of bodily pleasure. A single adjustment in Catherine's brain might realign her goals to be consistent with St. Joan's plans for a fitting edifice. "I should repair Catherine's brain."

As St. Joan reached out to calm the central hormone factory in Catherine's temple, a stronger force than Brother Richard stayed the action.

"Help," Catherine called out in ignorance of the real threat.

Mother rushed in. "What happened?"

Catherine was standing on the bed. "Something planned to snuff me out."

Mother reached up for Catherine's hand. "Not you, brightness. The Lord revels in His creation when He views you."

"You think so, do you?" Catherine's thoughts didn't feel very religious, down right pagan in fact.

"What did you dream?" Mother asked, stroking Catherine's hand.

'Nothing," Catherine placed her hand on her racing heart. "I awoke from danger."

"You're all right now; but you didn't eat supper." Mother said. "I couldn't get you awake then."

"I remember the dream," Catherine said. "It was a mysterious, miracle play in the old Refectory. Minstrels were playing their viols, trumpeting their horns, while shepherds piped their reed flutes and the pilgrims sang verses of the Chanson de Roland." Catherine kept hold of her mother's hand. "Some of the words were: 'How sweet the quietness at Domremy, against the wild alarms of Orleans, the long heartbreaking stays of Paris and Rheims' cruel treachery.'"

Catherine patted the bed and Mother sat next to her. "Mother, I probably should talk to you about not going to college."

"No, you should not!" Mother said, and then asked, "Was the Chanson similar to the Ode to Joy?"

"But, Mother...."

Tuesday, June 4th

After Catherine showered on Tuesday morning, ravenous for a breakfast of sausage and eggs, she hurried down the hotel's narrow stairs. She could be sipping her second cup of coffee by the time Mother got ready. More importantly, Anton wouldn't notice how rapidly she could inhale an entire plate of food.

But, Mrs. Bermont held the office half-door open in the foyer. Catherine prayed she would be quick. Her saliva glands were working overtime for breakfast. She danced toward the exit as they exchanged good mornings.

"Anton's changed his schedule for sketching your mother." Gail Bermont moved in slow motion. She played with a red satin ribbon on her bib apron, tying and untying it. Catherine hopped up and down at the door, as Mrs. Bermont finished a double bow and patted it down on her chest. "Anton...," Mrs. Bermont started.

"Yes, Anton?" Catherine prompted.

It was a muddled message. "Sister Josetta agrees he should start making arrangements." For what didn't get explained. Maybe it didn't matter. Catherine found it hard to concentrate on the dangling participles. Maybe her stomach growled enough to drown out some of the references.

Mrs. Bermont gave a dreamy-eyed rendition of the changed plans. "I couldn't be happier. He's going with Romèe to the convent on the mainland. Today, five years ago, he found her in the bay swimming away from the fishing boat."

Nobody's great love of sisters, nuns, or fishing, Catherine wasn't sure what Mrs. Bermont was talking on and on about. She didn't want to ask what happened to Anton so many years ago, even if it was a drowning nun. It was time to eat!

Then Mrs. Bermont seemed to wake up. She held out her arm to Catherine, who had the outer door open ready to jump down the steps to the street.

Across the street Catherine could see the glistening red enamel tables set with gay pots of geraniums and peaked napkins, waiting for her. She could smell the coffee.

Mrs. Bermont raised her voice to catch Catherine in mid-flight. "Anton plans to be through with the sketch before he goes."

Catherine thought she had focused long enough on the ginger bow to hear that Anton would sketch her mother before breakfast. Mrs. Bermont smiled in relief. Catherine thanked her, mostly for letting her run off to breakfast. However, as she stepped into the warm street, Catherine turned to ask Mrs. Bermont if Anton still planned to meet her in the Merveille's cellar.

The office door closed.

Catherine would check with Anton when he sketched Mother. The only syllable that stuck in an idle, non-hungry cell of her brain was the 'fore' part of the word 'before.' So, four o'clock still held the promise of at least an embrace with Anton, maybe their first kiss. On the hotel's staircase, when he made her promise to meet him alone, Anton seemed excited, even blushing.

After Catherine had downed her breakfast, Mother joined her in the restaurant. Beattles' music surprised the air. Mother cocked her head to hear it better and looked even younger in the softened light of the shaded arbor.

Romèe and Mrs. Bermont walked by hurriedly.

Romèe seemed loathe to go with his aunt, fixing his usual stare of appreciation on Catherine. "Anton has another beautiful model to sketch."

"Thank you," Mother said. "We're leaving in three days."

Gail Bermont merely nodded to them as she pulled Romèe away.

Waiting for Anton to appear at the hotel entrance, Catherine concentrated on the place she wanted to call her permanent home. The front door was painted a bright blue. The matching shutters and window boxes filled with blue hydrangea distracted her from the somber gray stones of the building. The lintel could have been a Roman stone stolen from some demolished temple. The round stone steps were a lighter shade of gray due to Anton's bleaching each day when he threw the scrub water down the two steps to sweep off any tourist litter.

Catherine wondered if that would be her job when they married. She could manage that. And she anticipated the click of her mother's tongue when she found out about the nude sketch. It went against her noblest intentions, that click. Mother could speak eloquently about free love, giving double messages about marriage: as immoral, even legal prostitution in a loveless match, while at the same time expounding on the virtues of a loving commitment. Nevertheless, anything shocking produced her mother's involuntary, censoring vocal click.

Anton waved when he came out of the hotel, but then marched down the street in the opposite direction.

Mother sipped her coffee, but Catherine watched as Anton slipped a drawing out of a large envelope as if for a last look, before he mailed it off. Catherine was sure the portrait sketch was of her.

When Anton joined them, he casually tipped up Mother's chin. "Lean a little forward, Mrs. Marksteiner."

"Call me Marie," she said. "Are you shadowing my turtle neck?"

"No, Madam. Your spirit shines forth," he said. "I am positioning the frame."

Mother laughed. "A gentleman!"

"And a scamp," Catherine couldn't help adding.

During the sketch Mother questioned Anton. He never once yelled at her for moving or talking. Anton seemed more at ease than he had been with Catherine. He chatted about his mother and friends. Obviously, Catherine's nudity *had* affected their modeling session.

Catherine knew how quickly a day could be exhausted. Filled with perfectly reasonable temptations, wasted hours could empty her dreams of the possibility of adding significant buildings to the world's faint traces of civilization. Catherine reached down next to Anton's chair to pull a pencil out of his sketch box. He noticed. "I need another sketch pad too."

Anton handed her an eight-by-twelve pad, then reacted to her obvious disappointment. "I have a newspaper-size pad I use for continuous-line drawings. I'll leave it outside your door before I leave for the mainland."

Catherine roughly laid out more ideas for the addition to the neoclassic facade of the cathedral. Part of the old abbey had fallen leaving a clearing one-eighth the length of the original structure. The island's rock foundations were leanest on the west side, so the addition would have to be light as air on the west platform.

A slight breeze brushed her hair away from her face. She could feel her guardian angel's wings on her shoulders, and a new happiness confirmed the building should be as dainty as one of Joan of Arc's butterflies.

At the breakfast table, Catherine listened to Anton charm her mother.

"Did you recognize the deep mourning clothes my mother wears?" Anton asked. "She's spent most of the last year in my father's greenhouse. It's on the roof of the hotel."

Mother sympathized. "My third husband died of a heart attack four months ago."

Catherine interjected, "Mother is going to remarry when she returns to America."

"In my own defense." Mother smiled. "Danny Passantino was the family lawyer. I hadn't gone out looking for a replacement."

Anton moved his chair closer to Mother almost forgetting his sketchpad in the process. "Isn't my mother an attractive woman?" Mother nodded. "She has a nice business, and she's been asked out."

Mother reassured him. "Mrs. Bermont will find someone, when she wants to." Anton showed them his finished sketch. Mother said, "I'm flattered."

The sketch showed Mother's beautiful hands to advantage. They were heavily ringed with the gifts from her dead husbands. Her sagging neck was hidden under a soft scarf and her hair, actually quite sparse, was presented as a curly halo. In the sketch Mother's age got lost in her expression of curiosity and delight.

Anton held the drawing in mid-air on its way to his satchel. "Perhaps you could talk to my mother," he smiled, "to influence her."

Mother said, "I'd be glad to try."

Anton rushed away before Catherine could remind him of their meeting that afternoon. Catherine looked at the lines of a dome on the sketchpad in her lap. No sense showing this to her mother. It didn't compete with Anton's flattery. Catherine closed the cover over her blob of a drawing.

Mother motioned for the waiter to bring their bill. "When was Anton a scamp with you?"

"He has nice manners, doesn't he?" Catherine stalled. "Don't you love his hair?" Catherine spread her arms wide to declare, "I love him."

In the process she knocked into the waiter's arm as he tried to refill her water glass. The waiter hastily retrieved the rolling glass and sopped up the water. Catherine crowed, "Now I'm baptized for the rites of love."

"Good hair is not a character trait a person could rely on," Mother said.

"He attracted me on the first day," Catherine said. "Did I tell you about his eyes? Usually I hate men without eyebrows or dark lashes. Anton's long blond lashes make me want to test my teeth on that surrounding pale ruff. I'm not afraid of sex. I intend to give myself to an entire person."

Mother smiled. "Yes, when you touch another human being, you have to be responsible for their feelings."

"I haven't met anyone I wanted to invest all that energy in, until Anton." Then Catherine asked, "Do I act like a virgin?"

"Deciding who to share your life with might take a little time."

"Anton appears able to wait for me to finish school, and he certainly honors his mother."

"By honoring his mother, do you mean taking over the family business?"

"I mean he can't marry while Mrs. Bermont remains in mourning."

Mother got downright sarcastic. "Doesn't believe in marriage?"

Catherine could see she wasn't gaining any ground. "You should have seen the way he sketched me."

"How did he sketch you?"

"Nude, behind the altar in the fantasy you told me about."

The click came. Mother dropped her pen as she was signing the check. She whispered, "In my fantasy, I make love behind the altar."

"Anton only sketched me."

Mother recovered enough to ask, "Did Anton touch you?"

Her mother seemed somewhat relieved that Anton had only tugged at Catherine's hair.

"The amoral behavior code of artists includes believing sex frees up their creative abilities. Whereas, well-defined limits improve an artist's abilities. A sketch has edges and a pencil only so much lead. Opening oneself to behavior society has proven to cause negative consequences only produces suffering to an otherwise difficult choice of careers."

Catherine grinned. Mother's words rolled off her. The click had said it all. Catherine had taken a step away from her mother towards womanhood. Nevertheless, Catherine tried to reason with her. "Didn't you teach me if I want something to ask for it? Well, I want Anton and now you are acting jealous, playing stupid, or staying stubborn." Mother shook her head. Catherine's voice dropped to a harsh whisper, "It is my life!"

Mother put her hands on her hips, and still sitting, swaggered like a naughty child, repeating a taunting game they had played a thousand times. "Who gave it to you?"

Catherine gave a new answer, "The Lord."

Mother wouldn't let go of the familiar script. "A believer, at this late date? I decided you."

Catherine wondered how many mothers were as childish, or confident enough to play as this silly, lovable mother of hers. Catherine bantered back, "You and who else."

"Forgot his name? Daddy!" Mother laughed. She took Catherine's hand. "I can't live it for you."

Here in this sheltered bay across an entire ocean from what she had recognized as home, Catherine felt closer to her mother than she had in all the months since Jimmy's death.

She closed her eyes for a second to recapture the feeling of being loved and loving wholeheartedly, which calmed her. A bank account of emotional stability, that's what Mother's love meant to her. She had a right to set foot anywhere, in any heart and claim it as her own.

Anton could be hers.

CHAPTER EIGHT

Romèe dragged his feet away from Catherine as she waited for Anton to sketch her mother. His heart felt like it was being torn out of his chest. She was such a lovely bird and Anton could hurt her so easily. Would hurt her. Romèe was sure of that.

Aunt Gail took his arm and prodded him with the words, "Artichoke House." She promised to influence the landlord to give the lease to him.

Romèe intended to lease the house for ninety-nine years. That would give him enough time on the Mont, hopefully with Catherine at his side. Three more days, her mother had said. Would he be able to convince Catherine not to leave Mont Saint Michel in three days?

Mr. Shaldenmere seemed skeptical of Romèe, but the small Frenchman's blue eyes twinkled at Aunt Gail, whose dignity refused any encouragement. After the successful negotiation, Aunt Gail paid a year's rent by check and promised her wealthy brother would provide his son, Romèe, with the rest of the hefty sum in two days.

They met Anton at the taxi stand on the causeway. At the train depot his mother gave them orders for Shelby, mainly that she should join them in Paris. When she hugged Romèe, she whispered, "I'll invite Catherine to supper to soften Anton's blow."

"If I didn't need to see my mother for the money, Anton could go alone," Romèe said, reluctant to leave.

"Nonsense," Anton said. "How will Sister Josetta let me in the convent by myself?"

"I'm afraid he's right," Aunt Gail said. "Tomorrow night Anton can keep the Inn and clear up anything I've been unable to say to Catherine. By Thursday, Catherine will be right as rain."

On the noisy train to Paris, the normally talkative cousins sat silently facing each other. The unspoken words felt like iron barbs in Romèe's throat.

"I'm sorry," Anton finally said. "I still claim I'm innocent, but how can I make you feel less miserable."

"She's too young," Romèe nearly spit the words out. "You should have known!"

"Romèe, young girls have these infatuations, I'm sure it's nothing serious. You still have a chance."

Romèe glared. "Why can't you admit you seduced her?"

"I didn't intend to," Anton said. "I thought she knew I was too old for her."

"Your attention, drawing every line of her body," Romèe coughed as the anger rose up in him. "Did. You did play with her affection."

"I admit she is immature." Anton smoothed the pleat on his trousers. "French girls would not take a modeling session so personally."

"She's American." Romèe wanted to hit something or sob. "They're open-hearted, trusting."

Anton reached to touch Romèe's knee, but a woman across the aisle turned to stare at them. Anton smiled sweetly at her, raising his voice to make sure she heard every word, "Catherine will love you in time. You're there for her. She just hasn't noticed."

Romèe pulled a hair out of his eyebrow in frustration. "When I talk, she doesn't even hear me."

"She hears you. You two are closer than you think. Right now your words seem to be her own. Give it time."

"You didn't need any time."

"I've learned my lesson. I'll straighten everything out."

"You realize you are going to hurt Catherine when you tell her you are engaged."

"Young girls recover quickly."

"She's more of a woman than you know." Romèe said and then lapsed into another tense silence.

Catherine checked the chip and battery in her camera. Her watch read 2:30. Plenty of time to photograph the Abbey's foundations. She set off up the steeper path to the Abbey starting at the Hotel de' Bermont's back alley. Down below, the Grand Rue was already clogged with tourists trapped by the unending vendor stalls. Only a few foot soldiers, adventuresome or lost, struggled beside her to climb past the graveyard.

Unusual, ninety-degree heat discouraged her from exploring the names on the stones. She took a picture of a tour guide explaining who was allowed to be buried in the small plot. Catherine had three more days to make sure she could be one of the lucky souls to be entombed on the Mont. Builders were allowed to lie eternally under this peaceful terrace. Eventually her grave would be filtered of its bones and piled hip-to-hip with the great ones in the tall storehouse of skeletons behind Saint Peter's parish church.

Catherine squeezed between a few of the gawkers and ended up on the guard walk to the Grand Staircase. A line of pilgrims with parish banners struggled up the steps. Catherine offered her arm to a faltering, heavy lady on her knees who waved her off. The discomfort was part of the woman's plan for salvation. Suffering was not in Catherine's book of saving graces. She did believe headaches were warning signs that all was not well, a clear signal to seek a harmony of the mind and body. If the fat lady had faulted her gluttony for the chest pains and aching calves instead of crediting her empty soul with the agony she was enduring, the very stones beneath her shoes would rejoice with the angels.

Aiming her camera at their pitiful faces, she realized they were the real foundation stones of the Abbey. Each creepy gray rock in Mont Saint Michel housed discarded sins of pilgrims who had climbed the Grand Staircase for their redemption. She noticed a rectangular iron chain discarded in a heap next to an anchor post under the first arch. *Forging their own chains,* she remembered from Scrooge's first haunt.

Catherine climbed to the porch between the Benedictine quarters and the west courtyard in front of the Abbey. More passengers had disembarked from a line of twenty buses parked alongside the causeway four stories below. Unconcerned sheep grazed on the salt-water marsh grasses. Their mutton servings were said to have the unique flavor of sea-salt.

The architect in her wanted the tourists to reach for the joy the Lord intended for their lives. But in the midst of chiding them, Catherine felt a twinge of envy for the crowds' cohesiveness, its solidarity, even as she disdained their herd mentality. She glanced up at the pinnacle to the stature of Saint Michael. His golden stance promised protection from lightning which in earlier centuries had destroyed towers and lit destructive fires. He surely must want these pilgrims to find joy in their lives.

Skirting the back of the nave as parishioners settled in for mass, Catherine found her way to a staircase leading down to the Romanesque vaulted substructure and Saint Martin's chapel under the south transept of the church. Following tourists down to the Crypt of the Gros-Piliers, she heard a guide describe the huge supports as giant sausages. "After the Romanesque church collapsed during the Hundred Years War, these granite shafts were built to bear the weight of the Gothic Choir above."

The pillars had the strength and elegance of elephant legs, content to carry the burden of the stained-glass hallelujahs sung in the soaring arched choir above them.

Communion was being served when Catherine returned to the church. Positioned against the cold wall, perpendicular to the glittering, robed priest, Catherine watched the pilgrimages from various parishes march down the main aisle. Barefoot friars hurried to dispense the consecrated hosts. The organ music, choir, and incense added to the heightened expectancy of the crowd. Reason was swept aside in the hope of touching prisoners of the unknown.

A robust young monk with cheerful eyes approached Catherine holding out the gold communion platter. She declined and the barefoot friar moved on, but Catherine burst into tears as the monk turned his back. Rejection was always a two-edged sword. She wanted to be a believer, to be a part of some overwhelming, lasting peace.

Embarrassed by her susceptibility to these religious rituals, she quickly crossed the back of the hall to the find the Merveille tour path. Maybe after Mother returned to the States, before marrying Anton, Catherine would convert from a non-religious life to one catholic with acceptance hurdles.

She continued her lonely, photographic tour of the Merveille down to the square-pillared cellar of the northern buildings. The supporting walls showed aging pieces of the original monastery destroyed by fire in the eleventh century. The unpopular cellar was where Anton promised to meet with her. Catherine's watch read 3:00. Way too early for Anton to be waiting.

Proceeding to the eastern section of the cellar, the Almonry, Catherine found the pillars half the size of the Gros Piliers. Their capitals were unadorned. Her guidebook explained the hall was accessible to the poor, an undecorated homeless shelter. Two fireplaces filled up one wall. A six-foot man could easily stand where the wood once blazed roasting entire joints of venison for the hungry visitors of the past.

In the Refectory above the Almonry, a gentle diffuse light filled the room. Originally, the floor was tiled and the walls painted. Until Catherine walked well into the hall, the source of the room's light was hidden. Windows at the eastern gable let in some light; but in order for the fortified wall to support the heavy framework of the dormitory above, fifty-nine narrower windows were set deep in the thick north and south walls.

Back in the basement of the Merveille, Catherine went through the Almonry again to gain access to the Knights Hall above the western cellar. There, three aisles were separated by narrow columns rising to graceful vaults. Two rows of columns with individually decorated capitals divided the ninety-by-sixty foot room. The elegant shafts were twenty-two feet high with the supports designed to hold the monks' cloister above it. Massive round-topped windows in the arching of the vaults provided light, while the two hooded fireplaces promised to furnish warmth.

The arched and covered architecture of the cloister above the Knights Hall provided a pleasant, sunny walk around the flowering garden. Catherine sat at the glassed-in west wall, watching people saunter among the gardens and terraces below. Once St. Joan's dome was constructed on the terrace below, tourists would enjoy butterflies floating over hanging gardens all year round. Strangers passed. How would they feel when they opened their guidebooks to read this was where she had designed the famous future marvel of France, the Dome of St. Joan?

Arrogance only knows one direction, and it is not further heights. Where had she read that? Catherine remembered walking to high school in a brand new outfit. She looked fine, but each step made a crunching sound. She realized her lunch sack was swinging into her books. She tucked it next to her chest and proceeded on, looking and sounding perfect. But, a raised portion of the sidewalk caused her to stumble and lurch forward. She had laughed aloud at getting kicked in the pants for her prideful stride. Fate consistently arranged similar circumstances to humble her regularly.

At 4:00 o'clock Catherine descended into the basement for the second or third time. The wind from the open door of the west exit chilled her. Bright flowers beckoned along a terrace wall. The cool fragrant breeze made her wish she'd brought her sweater.

Where was Anton? She'd been waiting for fifteen minutes. Five more and that would be it.

The caretaker of the hour pulled the east hall doors shut. He lit the hanging votive lamps in front of the sculpture of Saint Michael. The glass reflected red shadows onto the stone model of the golden stature at the top of the Mont. The devilish side of the archangel emerged. His eyes winked in the flickering red light and the stalwart mouth leered at her.

The caretaker lurked behind the pillars making his way to the exit, maybe to shut those doors, too. Catherine took a step to stop him, when the back of her neck felt a hand on it. She whirled around grinning; expecting to cuff Anton, but only air greeted her.

A sadness crept over her. She had wanted to be alone with Anton again. This time she'd planned to touch his hair. Maybe he was still on his way. She reached out her arms to hurry him along. Oh, to be embraced, to let their souls finally meet. Her arms dropped to her side. At least she wanted to look into his eyes and maybe be kissed.

Catherine moved away from Saint Michael's statue. There was no one else in the high hall. The red light danced before the statue.

The west door was still opened to the sky. She felt a great presence, a hollow thing, filling the hall.

'Okay,' she thought, steeling her nerves, 'So what or who are you?'

Overhead a white dove flew to one of the high window ledges. It fluttered its wings and settled more comfortably to rest.

"You're not much help." Catherine's small voice echoed.

Then she felt a rush of souls march right through her, their peasant terror nearly seen. In pursuit were swearing, clanking English marauders. She could smell their unwashed stench, the ferment on their breaths. She stamped her foot at the spirit nonsense. She wouldn't have it. They could find someone else to taunt.

She pulled her soul closer to her bones, sewing up her sensors, closing out the other realms. Catherine walked to the door and stepped out into a welcome patch of sun, alone.

CHAPTER NINE

When Catherine returned to the hotel, her mother was waiting in the upstairs hall. "Mrs. Bermont invited us to supper. Romèe and Anton are detained on some grand mission on the mainland."

In the fifteen minutes allotted for Catherine to dress, she insisted Mother listen to her latest haunting. "Joan of Arc must have experienced the same frightened mob of peasants being chased by that noisy English army."

"I wondered where you had disappeared." Mother grumbled, "For being known as a great ghost hunter, I've not had one inkling of ghostly activity."

"It was as if I were reliving the scene as St. Joan."

Mother said, "My head must be so filled with facts about the Maid I can't hear any of her movements."

"Shall I ask her anything for you?" Catherine finished brushing her hair.

"Just stay open for her. She needed quiet to hear her capricious voices. A solitary art, the mystics pursue peaceful silence to reach above the rest of humanity."

As Catherine and Mother descended the hotel stairs, Catherine invented Anton waiting nervously for them at the bottom. He would wink at Catherine and tug on the green scarf she had tied in her hair. Catherine thought she might float into the Bermont apartment. Even the sight of his mother's serious face, as they entered, didn't dampen Catherine's happiness.

Mrs. Bermont greeted them formally.

Catherine instinctively took a step back. In her romantic illusion, she would have stepped on Anton's toes. He would probably push her in the rump. Catherine couldn't help smiling broadly at that naughty thought.

Mother seized the moment to respond in the formal tone of her hostess. "It's very gracious of you to honor the whim of our silly children."

Mrs. Bermont said, "I think we have both raised clowns." She led them through the library-parlor. Crowded with bookshelves, the room was large enough for the grand piano which was topped with a zillion portraits in ornate silver and gold frames. At least twenty plants hung over a dozen musty, upholstered chairs.

Mrs. Bermont paused and turned back to them at the threshold of the dining room. "The place is crammed with the leavings of six generations of Bermonts. My wedding gifts are secreted away in closets and attics because the house was bulging when I arrived." Graciously motioning them to their places in the dining room, Mrs. Bermont added, "I meant to rid myself of some of it, but as soon as Anton was born I felt obligated to save everything for his family. Now the task of keeping all the stuff will be his."

"Anton won't like being relegated to a junk man," Catherine said.

Mother and Mrs. Bermont shook their heads at her impertinence.

In the high-ceilinged dining room, huge china cabinets claimed the four corners while an oversized, thick-legged, antique table dominated the small room. The only lighting in the windowless inner room came from lamps attached to oil paintings of ghoulish floral arrangements. Candelabras dripped wax on the scarlet table cloth.

Catherine half expected a crow to fly through the room repeating, 'Nevermore.' It was hard to stay cheerful in such a somber room. So, Catherine felt compelled to continue her imaginary world where Anton pulled out her chair, and whispered into her hair how nice it was to have a fresh fragrance added to the room. Catherine caught her mother's eye to see if she'd noticed Anton's sweet, pretend attentions made her blush.

Mother complimented Mrs. Bermont, "Gracious dining is a rare treasure."

The two women quickly began to address each other by their first names discussing the coriander sauce on the fish.

"It was a favorite of my late husband," Mrs. Bermont said.

Catherine knew Anton would have tried to chide his mother for bringing up the sad subject, but Mother encouraged her to talk.

Mrs. Bermont conceded, "Anton has heard all my ghost stories enough times."

Mother stopped eating. "You see your husband?"

"I only feel his presence in the greenhouse, mostly."

Catherine forgot about Anton's pretend presence and asked, "Does the ghost feel cold?"

Mrs. Bermont laughed. "I never feel cold when Gerard is around, dead or alive."

"I admit I have warm memories of two of my husbands."

"The greenhouse brings me closer to Gerard's spirit." Mrs. Bermont seemed ready to cry.

Catherine surprised herself by suddenly jumping up to hug Mrs. Bermont. Noticeably embarrassed by her rashness, Catherine awkwardly resumed her seat at the table.

Mother covered for her. "Thankfully none of my husbands haunt me. It would be rude to my next husband, if they decided to return at this late date."

Mrs. Bermont did not appreciate the joke, so Catherine added, "Mother believes when a partner dies, only one should give up living."

Mrs. Bermont said, "I liked what I had."

"The whole world is out there ready to be loved," Mother said.

"I can't face going through the loss again." Mrs. Bermont stirred the empty sauce bowl.

Turning to Catherine, Mother said, "I think the very words 'living' and 'loving' were originally the same statement."

Mrs. Bermont tried to shift the focus of the conversation by asking Catherine, "Where do you plan to be twenty years from now?"

Catherine touched her throat to swallow. "Will Anton still be living on Mont Saint Michel in twenty years?"

Catherine could hear Mother and Mrs. Bermont continue their conversation while she concentrated on visualizing Anton's hypnotizing eyes. He would stare at the painting over her head while he told her about a house near the Grand Staircase, with a view of the French coast, that he planned to fill with children. Catherine said that she liked kids. She had been listening on some level to Mrs. Bermont and her mother talk about how people, children stop loving.

Mother said, "Children always love their parents, they just stop being as charming about it."

"I think when children get busy arranging their own lives," Mrs. Bermont said, "there isn't enough energy left for parents."

"I want children," Catherine said.

Mrs. Bermont and Mother stopped talking for a moment to look at her, while they considered her statement.

Then Mrs. Bermont said, "When I first held Anton at the hospital, I thought we would be separated some day and I would never see him again."

Mother said, "When I saw how beautiful my Catherine was, I knew she would need me for the rest of her life."

"Is that need yours or Catherine's?"

In the meantime, Catherine's fanciful Anton reached across the table to touch Catherine's fingertips. "How many children would you like to have?" he asked.

Catherine thought 'what a nice way to propose.' She stammered over the simple word and it came out way too loud, "Eight!"

Smiling at Mrs. Bermont and her mother, Catherine thought, 'I'm home.' She examined the pattern of the silverware, the delicate china, the crystal. The walls would have to be repapered a light shade of blue. Standing lamps in the corners would help and those oils would have to go. Seascapes would be a nice addition. The garish table was campy enough to stay, if Anton insisted. The candelabras could use flickering battery bulbs. Catherine filled the empty chairs with curly redhead and blonde girls, but the boys, of exceptional intelligence, all had curly dark hair like Romèe's. Five children would do, three boys and two girls. Life would be sweet and staid.

In the background, Mother said, "When daughters marry, their mothers gain a son."

Mrs. Bermont cleared her throat and directed a query to Catherine, "Anton tells me you are studying to be an architect."

"You're probably wondering how I intend to design buildings while raising eight children." Catherine lightheartedly resumed eating.

"When they're sleeping?" Mrs. Bermont asked, serving her another portion of fish.

Catherine said, "Kahlil Gibran says that children only pass through their parents lives."

Mother said, "Each cell of a child was designed by the parental genes."

Mrs. Bermont was more interested in stating her theories than listening to rebuttals. "Perhaps parents pass through the beginnings of their children's lives. Children are merely output of the union."

Mother caught the isolating virus of giving a soliloquy in a crowd. "When I carried Catherine, I felt each cell of her growth as it opened another chamber in my heart, not only for my child, but for the whole world. Catherine was love's input."

Mrs. Bermont took their plates away and served each of them a tall glass of dessert fruit and custard.

Mother smiled at Catherine's delight. "When Catherine has finished college and married, I want to help her chose a china pattern and lay out the christening robes for her children."

Mrs. Bermont shook her head. "I want a life after children. I fed Anton, clothed him and now I want to put on fresh raiment."

Near midnight Catherine was awakened by her mother shaking her. Apparently she had cried out in her sleep about being lost.

"You and your ghost talk," Catherine grumbled. "Joan of Arc told me to go to Rome, no Romèe!"

Mother sat down on the bed. "What was St. Joan wearing?"

Catherine had to laugh. "Here I receive a clear message and you only want to know the details of her dress."

"I know the historical wardrobe of the Maid," Mother insisted, "and I want to be sure the message is from her."

Catherine humored her. "A coarsely woven dark red dress. I could see the white collar and hem of a garment under it."

Mother whispered in awe. "The women of Lorraine wore red skirts."

"Joan wore men's clothing or armor."

"After she left her hometown. Don't you remember the painting by Gauguin where Joan of Arc, dressed as a village maid, stands under the sacred beech tree listening to her voices?"

Catherine sat up in bed. "This girl looked like Lisa Mannelli. You know those popping black eyes and full lips. Should I go to Rome?"

Mother reminded her, "The word was Romèe not Rome. Romèe means someone who makes a pilgrimage to Rome. It's a person, male or female, not a place. Joan of Arc's mother was called Romèe for that reason. Anton's cousin must have a part in building your Dome. Let's figure it out in the morning."

Alone in the hotel's Queen of Hearts room, Catherine wondered if she qualified as a candidate in need of psychological counseling. Maintaining a fantasy world with Anton was diverting, but was it healthy? These nightmares imposed by her mother's suggestions could be a symptom of trying to hold onto her mother. Would she go completely insane as soon as her mother left her to marry Danny?

Her mother refused to believe Anton was enough of a factor in her life to quit college before she attended one class.

Catherine floated off to sleep wondering how old Joan of Arc was when her mother made a pilgrimage to Rome. It had to be before she was sixteen, maybe when St. Joan had refused to marry. Would a mother feel guilty raising a daughter who hated her role, enough to travel to Rome? St. Joan's mother testified at her sainthood hearings, twenty years after St. Joan's martyrdom at the stake. The mother may have organized the campaign at the King's bidding. Had St. Joan's mother made enough friends in that earlier trip to Rome to help in her lay siege against the Church to gain her daughter's sainthood?

Could St. Joan's parents have been at odds? Catherine thought she had read in the heresy trial that St. Joan's father accepted a dowry from the boy who claimed St. Joan was his betrothed. Maybe he needed the funds to pay protection to the English marauders.

In the dream prompted by her thoughts, Catherine could see St. Joan's parents in a low dark kitchen standing toe to toe.

Isabelle Romèe had her hands on her hips, feet spread as if waiting for a familiar cuffing. Joan of Arc's father raised his hand and Romèe made the sign of the cross. His hand stayed posed in the air, forehead sweating, eyes bulging. Jacque didn't strike. Perhaps St. Joan's mother deemed the unweiled blow a miracle and went off to Rome in further defiance. Joan of Arc had to learn courage somewhere.

Wednesday, June 5th

Catherine heard Anton's knock early on Wednesday morning. He slipped her a giant sketch pad, colored pencils, a thermos, and a huge cup of sweetened coffee with cream. Then he put his finger on his lips to be quiet, shut the door, and left!

Catherine was hoping for a kiss.

Instead, Catherine plugged in her lunch-box sized printer inserting the latest chip from her camera into the printer. The photograph paper cost a lot of packing space, but happily her mother insisted Catherine would need every box. After triggering the print mechanism for four of the shots of the Merveille's western buildings, Catherine spread Anton's sketchbook open on the bed and laid out the courtyard where the original parts of three different naves had fallen.

Tourist books of the Mont helped with the exact dimensions. The cistern placement near the Merveille side of the Abbey would aid the watering system that Catherine had not completely solved. She put the pump houses and drainage motor enclosures right up next to the church face.

Then she realized the neoclassic facade would be hidden, so she redesigned the Dome's foundations in the middle of the courtyard directly below the cloister window, where the garden walk existed. She added a stone gazebo for the baptismal font. Inside the lattice structure, a marble christening bowl would be set atop a stone lily. Then Catherine worried over the structural braces for the glass dome.

About an hour later Mother came into Catherine's room through the bathroom. "When did you talk Anton out of more pencils?"

Catherine bit her pencil trying not to break her concentration. "He also left us a thermos."

Coffee in hand, Mother pulled up a chair to watch Catherine sketch. "It looks like a greenhouse."

"Exactly!" Catherine said, "With trellis frames."

"It's gorgeous. A Crystal Palace with Babylon's hanging gardens."

"I'm having trouble with the defrost and drainage lines. I need them all to be transparent." But Catherine was pleased and asked, "Do you know any billionaire Frenchman?"

Mother mentioned, "The Pope."

"He's from Argentina?"

"What does Romèe's father do for a living? Will the Dome be a butterfly sanctuary? How many times have I told you the fable when Joan unfurled her war banner, a cloud of butterflies followed?"

"It might as well serve as a year-round tourist trap."

Mother poured herself another cup of coffee. "When did you get the ideas?"

"Since I stepped on the island, I felt the empty space needed something; or from the dream of the diamond on my hand with its flowering world of butterflies and Joan of Arc trimming her sacred tree."

"I wondered how it all connects to the Romèe message from St. Joan."

Then Catherine remembered, "I was thinking of Anton, only he changed into the younger, Romèe with his black, curly hair. If someone could finance this, I could stay on the Mont without marriage."

"Usually a first love is not your last."

Already tense from the initial interruption, Catherine flared up. "Just because you are sexually adventurous doesn't mean your daughter would be. Anton's mother had only one love." Catherine played with the ends of her hair, sweeping her hair over one shoulder, teasing it over the drawings, absentmindedly plaiting it.

"I think you can see Gail's behavior isn't healthy," Mother said. "Do you want your hair braided?"

Catherine's frustrated hormones reacted. She threw Anton's pencils across the room. "It's not healthy to love?" She wanted to scream but she got off the bed to retrieve the pencils.

"It's not healthy to *not* let go, when your lover is dead."

"Anton loves me now," Catherine said.

"Anton hasn't mentioned he loves you to Gail." Mother put her chair back. "I think I'll take some pictures for Danny. I could use some company."

Catherine hugged her, encouraging her to go. "I'll be right here drawing."

After eighteen years, constantly at her mother's side, Catherine didn't have to be with her to know exactly what would follow. Mother would throw on a necklace and hat, grab her camera, turn left outside the hotel and proceed up to the Abbey. She always checked her watch, ten o'clock. Her camera would swing aimlessly at her side.

Finally, Catherine might have time to put all her ideas down on paper. Only two days left to make an indelible impression on Anton.

She laid the sketch books out on the floor. First she drew outlines of intricate glass structures modeled after the decorative stone spires of the Gothic Church, but glass would be too fragile to sustain their delicate peaks in seasonal storms.

Discouraged, Catherine stopped drawing, walked toward the mirror and brushed out her hair.

She thought of her mother getting overheated and sitting on the shady steps, fanning herself with her hat. Mother's multi-ringed hand would catch in her necklace, as it always did, and the multi-colored beads would roll down the steps, but her mother wouldn't chase them.

Staring at her first drawings of the Mont, Catherine carefully separated her hair and started to plait it into a French braid.

In the slickest tourist guide, an aerial shot of the Mont zoomed down to an ant-sized Saint Michael, who was transformed on the next page into a giant, a radiant gold knight of goodness against evil guarding the Mont for centuries from the perils of the encroaching sea.

Catherine wondered who her protector was. She checked her mirror image.

The giant shadow of her mother proceeded to climb the stairs to the Abbey, frightening a stray sparrow. Mother would have to sit down again before she reached the church door.

When a town person or early tourist walked by, Mother fiddled with her camera to cover her exhaustion. Mother was more shy than aloof.

Catherine kept her beginning braid in place with a rubber band before starting a new sketch. With her hair out of the picture, Catherine found the mirror reflected her thoughts more clearly. She could almost see her mother's progress.

Catherine awoke from half-heartedly dozing to hear a buzz of conversation from the restaurant below, even an occasional clinking of dishes. The white fluffy pillows and shams from the bed cushioned her back and head. She didn't quite remember pulling them down to the floor and checked to see if any were smudged from her pencils. What a strange productive day.

How long had she been drawing? Catherine thought she had been absently doodling, thinking of her mother's pilgrimage, but instead was surprised to find a domed edifice on her sketch pad. It fit snugly against the cellar of the Merveille. More importantly, inside the dome she had drawn faceted diamond shapes, giving it the look of an engagement ring's jewel set in the pinnacle outlines of Mont Saint Michel. The diamond structures were braces for rose, she decided, panels of glass.

Catherine spread her hands over the final sketch. Surely she hadn't drawn this. Her shoulders did ache from the session and the red indentation on her third finger told her the shortened pencils strewn on the carpet had been held by her, but these marvelously detailed renderings were far beyond her usual attempts.

The embodiment of an idea was always exciting. Would her talent be wanted if she didn't get an authorized degree? The drawings wouldn't change, but people trusted certified architects. She could live with doing this every day.

Catherine tried to rub the bump out of her index finger. If she drew this well, maybe school wouldn't be that difficult, and if drawing used up all her free time, maybe she could survive, alone.

This was architecture.

Not only did the drawings surprise Catherine at the degree of design talent, but they carefully depicted the idea of a glass building worthy of the Saint's fame.

Maybe her own need to fill the vacuum left by her goal to live on the Mont had been filled with this career answer for staying tied to the island architecturally. Mother admonished that only when a person can transcend daily cares could their destiny be determined.

Surely Joan of Arc's Dome at the Mont would shape her future. She traced a line of the dome with her fingernail. Faint odors from the colored smears on her fingertips convinced her. She could do this, unaided. A burst of joy hit her. This art would always be a part of her.

Catherine wished her mother would return. She rushed to the mirror, inspecting her braid. And, what happened to the morning? Light filled the Queen of Hearts room with the afternoon sun. The rosewood frame of the old mirror glowed. Its surface quivered as Catherine's attention honed in on her mother's tour.

Mother wandered among the columns of the Gothic Choir, sat down to read her tourist guide, and then took pictures of the seagulls flying up from the courtyard by the Cloister, finally wending her way back to the main altar.

Mother knocked gently on Catherine's door.

Opening it, Catherine embraced her. "Come and see what I've done."

Mother sat down on the floor and started to cry when she saw the drawings. "I'm feeling sorry for myself. Gail was right; you are growing up and away from me."

"Impossible," Catherine said. "Who will know when I'm faking it or when I'm real? I figured your beads broke and a sparrow flew up at your feet. After you sat down on the altar steps, I stopped watching."

"Watching?" Mother asked. Catherine found herself pointing at the mirror. "You should have kept an eye on me," Mother said. "A seagull flew into the church and landed at my feet." Mother took off her hat. "And, the bird talked to me."

Catherine's eyes widened in disbelief but her mother disregarded her reaction.

"I want to tell it as it happened," Mother said. "First the gull asked if I was napping. I said I had been crying."

The bird said, "Cut it out. I'm here."

So, I said, "Sure a big help you'll be after you vanish."

The seagull strutted around. "I could be the Maid's spirit."

"I tried to pick it up, but it disappeared."

"It was hot," Catherine said. "Did you doze off?"

"Of course not," Mother said. "That Father Damion, you told me about, came by."

"Are you the mother of the young girl who posed here?" he asked. "I cautioned them about the tourists coming."

Mother said she swore at him. Catherine laughed. Her mother was acting like a naughty child again.

Then the priest asked, "Are you a fallen-away Catholic."

Mother grinned. "I did a perfect pratfall for him."

Father Damion had laughed, but Mother wasn't going to let him off that easily. "I told him, 'You do more harm than good.'"

He defended himself, "I do a little good."

"Very little," Mother had said. "When I left the church, it seemed appropriate to kick the door. I had to limp home. You know there is a Chapel of Saint Catherine between the Abbott's lodgings, according to the guide book, but you can't visit it. It's very old. St. Joan could have made a pilgrimage to the Mont during the Hundred Years War to two of her Voices. And," she took a need breath before telling Catherine, "You'll be happy to know, I met Anton's mother on the way in and we've been invited to tea."

Catherine wanted to study her crystal palace, not attend a boring tea. Of course, if Anton were interested in her, she'd have to learn to like Mrs. Bermont someday. She didn't know enough about her to like or dislike her. Catherine put away her drawings.

Maybe Anton would walk through the rooms, even stay for a while.

For the tea Mother wore orange stretch pants, a long white tunic, with an orange and white scarf tied in a sailor's knot. Her blonde-gray hair was still wet from the shower and remained tightly curled. Mother refused to change, despite Catherine's protest, and even added orange hoop earrings.

Catherine wore a long blue dress. They didn't look, in Catherine's opinion, as if they should both be allowed in the same room. "You clash." Catherine stamped her foot.

"It's good for Gail to see a grown woman dress casually. Don't give it a second thought. Young girls always look informal."

Perhaps Mrs. Bermont could appreciate their different moods, but why couldn't her mother at least try to be regal when Catherine wanted her to be.

Mrs. Bermont escorted the mother-and-daughter team up to her second floor sitting room. The tea table sat in the bay window with a view of the horde of tourists below. The floor-level window ledge was filled with potted daffodils, tulips and hyacinths, all reaching for the sun. Luckily, the small table's lace cloth covered Mother's orange gym shoes.

Catherine sat on the edge of a small divan half filled with a stack of florist books. Their hostess poured tea in delicate china cups decorated with spring flowers. Iced cakes decorated with rose buds tempted Catherine more than once.

Mrs. Bermont turned to Catherine across the small room. "I remember asking where you will be in twenty years, but I don't remember the answer."

"Mother wants me to live a block away with a flock of redheaded kids." Mother stuck out her tongue. Catherine asked Mrs. Bermont, "May I page through these books on flowers?"

"Please browse," Mrs. Bermont. "My sister-in-law sent them to me. She's retiring and asked me to consider buying the business. Romèe wants to start an outlet here on the Mont for me."

Catherine perused the books looking for sturdy flowering plants that could exist on their own. She could guarantee they would have automatic sun and water. The pruning, fertilizing and providing of additional soil would have to be a once-a-year job with temporary scaffolding stored to accomplish it. Philodendrons didn't flower, but they could provide consistent greenery. What the dome needed was a florist on the island.

Catherine almost interrupted to ask Mrs. Bermont to repeat her news about Romèe's flower outlet; but then she heard her mother comment Anton wanted her to influence Gail. Mrs. Bermont wiped her fingertips on the napkin in her lap and tried to change the subject.

When Catherine tuned in to the conversation across the sea of books in her lap, she noticed they were carrying on parallel conversations again. They sounded more interested in what they each were saying again, than in what they were hearing. Catherine wanted to stop them to ask if they had just heard the other person's last comment. Engrossed in their own words, it was impossible to intrude.

Mother said, "I think you are helping me. Even though Anton wants you to end your mourning, Catherine wants me to let her go."

Mrs. Bermont said, "I was surprised to hear Americans don't wear black after the funeral day."

"I started to date my husband's lawyer after only four months."

"Father Damion told me it was a personal decision," Mrs. Bermont said. "I wanted to demonstrate by my example for Anton that my husband, Gerard, and I loved each other."

"He misunderstands," Mother said.

"He thinks I don't love Shelby?" Mrs. Bermont asked.

"Shelby? He thinks you want to keep him for yourself."

Who the heck was Shelby, Catherine wondered. Mrs. Bermont sat looking in her teacup without speaking. The silence grew. Catherine kept her nose in the flower book, hoping she would find out more by not joining the conversation.

Unfortunately, Mother changed the subject. "Our hotel rooms are beautifully decorated, especially Catherine's Queen of Hearts' room."

"I decorated it for Shelby," Mrs. Bermont said. "I wanted a daughter, but Anton had his own ideas."

Mother commented again, "It is a beautiful room."

Catherine could tell her mother wanted her to pitch in. But, Catherine deliberately turned a page. The room felt awkward. One of the books next to Catherine slid off the pile and fell to the floor.

Mrs. Bermont watched Catherine pick it up and then turned back to Mother, choosing to talk about Mother's search for Joan-of-Arc on the Mont. "Have you seen the ghost you are tracking?"

"So far, Catherine has had the most encounters with the Maid in her dreams. She's supposed to go to Romèe."

"My nephew, Romèe Laurent? He told his father since Catherine stepped on the Mont, he's been dreaming of the Pucelle. Apparently, Liza Minnelli resembles the girl in his dream."

Of course, Anton's cousin would claim anything to get closer to Catherine; but Romèe could serve as a florist for the Dome's upkeep.

Mrs. Bermont continued, "Romèe loves the Mont. Today he leased the Artichoke House. He says your daughter is interested in becoming a citizen too."

"Catherine?" Mother asked. "Is Shelby your sister-in-law?"

Mrs. Bermont laughed. "No. My sister-in-law's name is Bernie. Bernice's flower shop is in Pairs. I haven't actually seen it yet."

Mother said, "I'd love to see it with you."

They agreed to take an early train from Avranches, the next morning.

Then Mrs. Bermont asked, "Would you like to see the dress I'm making for them?"

Catherine got mixed up with all those cousins and aunts. She excused herself to return to her drawings; but she should have gone with them to see the dress Mrs. Bermont had made. Laying eyes on that dress would have saved her a lot of grief, tears and hair pulling.

CHAPTER TEN

Thursday, June 6th

Thursday morning Mother knocked on Catherine's hall door, poking her head in while Catherine was still in bed. "I just wanted to say, I'm late for the train. I'll explain later. Be back tomorrow." Mother paused, so Catherine sat up in bed.

"Gail and I talked all night," Mother said. "I see the pizza arrived. You will be all right. Just remember what I told you about first loves. The word 'first' is the operative term."

Catherine heard Mrs. Bermont call, and her mother hurried down the stairs to meet her.

It was still dark outside. Catherine struggled to the door, opening it just in time to hear the outer hotel door slam shut. Tomorrow? What had happened? It was way too early in the morning to decipher Mother's illogical words or actions. Maybe her mother told Mrs. Bermont how Anton loved her! Maybe the mothers of the bride and groom were off shopping in Paris for a surprise engagement present!

Catherine dressed quickly. She needed coffee.

One thing was clear s would have Anton all to herself for one day and one exploratory, un-chaperoned night. Mother was the wisest of woman.

When Anton finally opened the office's half-door to Catherine's insistent pounding, she asked him, "Have our mothers gone shopping?"

"They're visiting Aunt Bernie," he said, "in Paris. They'll likely take in opera tonight."

Catherine threw herself on the half-door's desk and hugged Anton's neck. "She likes you."

Anton kissed her forehead. "I'm glad to hear it, but you have to get down before a customer comes in."

Catherine sprung backwards off the counter with her arms spread wide. "What customers? It's just you and me kid!"

He admitted that was true. "I'll cook for us. Would you like that?"

"Absolutely, I'm ready for you!"

"I don't think my fish gumbo is that good. I have to finish some accounting work. Can you keep yourself occupied until about seven?"

Catherine was a little put-off by the delay, but quickly recovered for her pride's sake. "I'll print out my shots of the Abbey. I might have to add a few of the foundation work under the west platform, if I don't have every angle."

The day was long, lonely.

After securing breakfast from across the street, Catherine reviewed her sketches of Mont Saint Michel. Her career choice was delineated by these superb renderings of the dream of adding a pink crystal dome to the Mont. With formal classes to pass the certification requirements, her future was secure.

Now all she had to do was nail Anton's heart to her own and life would no longer include one lonely hour.

As the little printer spit out her photographs, Catherine spread the pictures out on the floor, next to the sketches. Her memory of the dimensions of the Abbey was exact in every instance.

She waited for the next print, and imagined babies rolling on the floor among the pictures and sketches. Sweet tow-headed cherubs, some with curly black hair filled every space on the rug. All hers. All the glory, all the love she would need in the world, hers for the asking. The Lord was good.

St. Joan pulled Brother Richard through the mirror behind Catherine. "I know I am not supposed to bother her, but she did mention my name."

"You cannot be straying back here every time a tourist mentions your name when they visit your Dome. Heaven is waiting for us," Brother Richard couldn't help grumbling, "and I for one am ready to attend."

"I will stay around until the Dome is completed," St. Joan insisted. "Romèe needs to be convinced as well as his father."

"Who will convince the French government or the Pope to approve the plans even if the money is available?"

"You know who," St. Joan said. "I have been the Lord's successful envoy in the past and my services are still needed."

"Have you considered that we might be stuck in this Purgatory of your designing to convince you of your inordinate sin of pride?" Brother Richard asked, but took a big step back into the safer realms behind the looking glass when St. Joan glared at him.

St. Joan kissed the top of Catherine's head, before she reluctantly, but not humbly followed her confessor.

Later that night when Catherine let herself into Anton's domain and found the kitchen, Anton had three huge pots boiling at once. He was cooking fish, cleaning them in two pots and popping pieces into another kettle big enough to feed thirty.

Catherine knocked on the side of the kitchen door.

"Go away!" he yelled, before he saw her. "Oh baby, come in." Anton threw a worried smile in her direction. "We may never eat." He had made the dish only once but could not remember all the ingredients.

"You've made way too much," Catherine said.

Anton wiped his sweating forehead with a dishtowel then threw the towel on the floor under the sink. "It just seems to keep growing."

Catherine opened a lid to smell the soup. "Have you tasted it?"

Anton took a spoonful. "Definitely needs something. I put enough salt in." He got a clean spoon, stirred and gave it to Catherine to taste.

Curry was missing they decided. After the seasoning was added, Anton claimed it was a miracle. "We might eat yet. Are you allowed to drink wine?"

"Yes, because Mother isn't here."

Anton turned the gas down and vented the soup's lid. Catherine struggled with the corkscrew until Anton took over.

Catherine had time to look around. "Why are the ceilings so high?"

"The incline of the hill back here and the floor above had to be squared off."

"So the entrance is really a half-story up." Anton cleaned up and put away his spices while Catherine surveyed the maps lining the upper half of three walls. "The Mont must be as far as St. Joan could get in France from Rouen's stake."

"I think you're right," Anton said bundling trash out the back door. "Has your mother found her ghost, then?"

"Apparently, I'm the target." Catharine said, hoping St. Joan missed her cue this time. St. Joan did seem to develop into a real presence whenever her name was mentioned. "Mother thinks St. Joan has taken over my hopes of becoming an architect to design a Dome for her."

"Have you?" Anton asked.

"Almost." Catherine perched in the middle of the room on a convenient stool, spinning on its cushion as Anton marched around the mammoth kitchen slamming pots and cupboard doors, dripping water all over the floor. When they had children, she could teach him to quiet down, and wipe up after himself. "Why don't you think St. Joan visited here while she was alive?"

Without breaking his stride in cleaning up the place, Anton said, "There is no evidence."

"But the Cardinal could have demanded everything to be destroyed. He was silent at her trial."

"Why would she risk coming here?" Anton asked. "See that label on the main map. This was English Nomandie."

"She came as a pilgrim to the French Mont to hear her Voices after Rheims. Saint Michael and Saint Catherine."

"Never happened," Anton said.

"Joan of Arc imperiled her body more than once to save her soul."

St. Joan hung in the mist above the rattled cook and Catherine. She motioned for Brother Richard to take note. "Two counts against Anton already. He makes entirely too much noise and he is dead wrong."

"Admit the truth," Brother Richard chided his ghostly mate, "You prefer Romèe because of his name."

"My mother was a brave and loyal saint," St. Joan said. "Without her services to the King to have my name redeemed…"

"He would have been anointed to his office by an unholy devil," Brother Richard said before taking to his heals. St. Joan wasn't one to be teased. Took herself way too seriously as far as Brother Richard was concerned.

"And I can be violent when provoked, as the English well know," St. Joan said as she chased the rascal out of the scene.

Catherine continued their discussions about Joan of Arc as Anton led the way to his mother's sitting room. He had set the table with candles and flowers. Catherine was impressed with the effort he was making for her. "And Mother thought you didn't love me."

Anton stumbled, as he attempted to sit down on the small couch. His wine glass spilt a little on the knee of his trousers. "Didn't love you? But then, everyone loves you."

Catherine confidently sat next to him, scooting the flower books over to make enough room and sipped her wine. "I love the wine and your company." Moving closer, she reached out her hand to rub the spot on his knee where he had spilled wine.

Anton jumped up. "I forgot to mail my letter to Shelby," he hurriedly said. "Let's walk down to the corner, then we'll check on the soup."

There was that name again. Another cousin, no doubt. Downstairs Catherine put her arm through Anton's as they made the short march to the corner. She chatted away, "Most of my photographs turned out well."

Anton freed his arm to mail a letter and apologized, "I'm sorry I haven't been listening." Catherine prattled on about the prints, knowing his attention seemed fixed on other subjects. Finally he said, "I'm glad our mothers have gone to Paris. It is the first time Mother has been off the island since Father died. Now I can give you the benefit of my full attention."

A thrill went through Catherine's slight frame. So this was how it would begin, in the throes of excitement.

Anton opened the hotel's door. "I've been meaning to get you alone to explain."

Everything in life was happening just as Catherine had hoped. Her art was secure and this full-grown, mature man was at her beck and call. After checking on the slowly cooking soup, they carried bread and cheese back upstairs with a second bottle of wine. Catherine did not want to tell him she thought she'd had enough of the wine for all practical purposes. He needn't try so hard to seduce her. She tried to join him on the couch again, but he moved to sit in one of the table's side chairs.

Expecting the best, Catherine thought he would approach her eventually. In some slight moment of hospitality between lighting a candle or passing her the salt, unencumbered, he would surely fall upon her. He would sweep her into his arms, as in that painting of the piano teacher kissing his fainting student. A compliment of hers, some insight or wit would stir his being into showing his appreciation for her uniqueness.

Maybe he would fall on his knees beside her and lay his sweet head in her lap. While she played with his blond curls he might caress her knees, slip his hand up. No, she would have to push him away then.

Catherine remembered a mating pair of pigeons she had watched the year before when she was much less mature. The male was ready to mount, but the female objected. The male tried again but the female nearly flew away. Convinced he was rejected, the male paced a bit and then brooded with his back to her. The female hadn't flown away and looked back wondering why he had not persisted. Then she went to him, nudged him, and cooed into his ear. Elated he plunged at her and they flew away for privacy.

Men were delicate creatures.

She would have to wait upon Anton's moods and moves. Catherine promised herself not to be discouraged if he found only a word or two to express his desire. She remembered Hemingway's description of the throat of his hero swelling with passion. Perhaps she should touch Anton first. She could pat his elbow or back and show her affection and encourage him to make the first move, she hoped.

"Mother understands you have to wait to marry me until your mother is out of mourning."

Anton stood up and came over to her, taking her hand. "Oh, Catherine, I have to tell you something."

Catherine appreciated his seriously lowered Hemingway tone. "Don't look so down." She smiled encouragingly. "I have to finish school, but four years will fly now that we can count on each other."

Anton began to sweat even though the kitchen's heat was well below them. He worriedly paced the room. "Come into my bedroom," he said. "I have to show you something."

Catherine was a little surprised when he left abruptly. She gathered her courage and followed him across the hall to his bedroom. Anton sat on the bed with his back to the door, so she started to unbutton her black lace blouse.

Anton turned with a picture frame in his hand. "No, stop. I have to explain." He raised the photo for her to see.

Catherine came around to his side of the bed. She sat down and put her hand on his knee.

"The girl in the picture is nobody's daughter. Seven years ago, when her stepfather drunkenly tried to rape her, she had to jump off their fishing boat just outside the bay of Mont Saint Michel. I found her and she let me name her, Shelby Constance -- after Shelly's poem the Constant Lover."

He handed Catherine the framed picture.

"Found her?" Catherine only nodded in response; her stomach had started to hurt.

Anton took the picture and placed it back on his nightstand. He traced the outline of the girl's face with his fingertip. "Now she lives in a convent on the mainland."

Catherine reached across Anton's lap to take the photo into her hands, remembering the day Mrs. Bermont had excitedly given her a message about a Sister Josetta and Anton fishing something out of the bay. This girl was the prize.

For all she'd been through the elfin-faced child maintained an open smile. Her dark mass of curls slipped over the shoulder of a blue shirt. Heavy brows highlighted slightly slanted eyes. It was a pleasant enough face and could not understand why she felt a lurking undertow.

"She joined a convent," Catherine said, replacing the frame. Much relieved, Catherine touched Anton's shoulder, but he pushed her away.

Then in quick apology, Anton took her hand. "She wouldn't tell them who her father was. We took care of her."

Catherine made a move to kiss his hand, but he ran out of the room again.

She followed Anton up a flight of back stairs to the roof. Her senses seemed locked in the confusion.

As the cool night air refreshed her, Catherine felt a wave of homesickness for the steamy smells of fish soup.

A glassed-in greenhouse filled half of the roof area. Anton swung its door open and heard the crash as the door hit the wall breaking its upper window.

Catherine approached as if disembodied.

Anton had turned on the lights; the plants glistened through the damp glass.

Then Catherine smelled the musky odor she associated with Joan of Arc in her dreams. The Saint must be near. Catherine felt her way blocked by the ghost.

"Fit that to Mont Saint Michel. Build my Dome for me," she heard Joan of Arc in her thoughts, the voice low, strident in its command.

Catherine nodded to the unseen presence and she was able to proceed. As she bent to pick up the shards of glass, Catherine could smell the fresh flowers growing in the greenhouse. She hoped there would be butterflies, but worried about the broken door. They might escape.

Looking up, she saw Anton standing in the doorway offering his hand. He beamed with happiness.

Catherine took his hand, thankful the storm was over. "So this is where your mother mourns for your father." This was where time held Anton in its grip.

"Mother's been working," Anton explained gesturing behind him to a beautiful wedding dress.

Catherine circled the beaded dress. "She didn't know my size," she said. "It's too small."

Anton put his arm gently around her shoulder. "Catherine, it's for Shelby."

Catherine gripped his arm. For a fleeting moment she hoped the girl was marrying someone else, but she already knew.

"I thought Mother was delaying my marriage," Anton said.

Catherine started to cry. "And mine."

CHAPTER ELEVEN

atherine managed to sit through the dinner of fish soup. Anton put his arm around her shoulders whenever tears could not be controlled. The soup was good and it settled her stomach, somewhat. She concentrated on her meditation breathing exercises while he talked.

On and on about Shelby. "We've written to each other every day for years, planning every minute of our future together."

Somehow, Catherine managed to convince him she was fine. "Mistakes happen in life. I'm just a little tired."

Composed, she returned his pledge of friendship and with a hug assured him all was well, whispering something polite about his happiness with Shelby. Mostly she just wanted to bolt.

As soon as Catherine shut the Bermonts' office door to the hall, she ran down the steps and away from the hotel windows. She could walk around the Mont until she really calmed down. Mother said walking was the best thing to do when you couldn't think straight, something about wheels not spinning in place. Not one constructive thought emerged from her present funk, a state of utter confusion and embarrassment.

"Oh, Lord," she prayed, "Please help me. I'll die."

"Of what, stupidity?" Came her own answer. How could she have been so confident a few hours ago and so destitute now? For that matter, how could an eighteen-year old be so deaf, dumb and blind?

When she reached the Chapel of Saint Aubert, Catherine decided to strike out for the isle of Tombelaine on the northern side of Mont Saint Michel. It didn't look far. Its outline was clear against the bright evening sky. She turned to look back at the Mont. No problem. The lights from Avanches provided enough background. Saint Michael's shining statue rose above the floodlights, showing the Merveille peaks to their best advantage.

Fortunately, the mud was fairly sturdy. Her gym shoes would be a wreck, but they could be washed. She couldn't get lost if she tried. She felt lost, wishing she had asked her mother about that flashlight. It seemed a hundred years ago, when Joan of Arc sent the lilies of France into her mother's room.

After half an hour, the Tombelaine Island did not seem any closer. Her socks were getting wet from the muddy bay. Was she walking in the flood tide or ebb tide?

Something flew by, a bird, or worse a bat.

Catherine turned too quickly to look behind her, and fell on her back in the slippery mud. Her head didn't hurt from the slushy bed, but her hair was a mess. She got to her knees, brushed thick mud from her hands onto her jeans. Her hair was weighted down with gluey muck.

A nobody's daughter, Shelby Constance, had won the day. Now she, Catherine, was nobody's sweetheart. The old song hung in her head. She whispered the ditty to herself, "I'm nobody's sweetheart, now."

She recalled Shelby's photo exactly. The cheekbones set in early sadness, the dark curls lush on her young shoulders. Shelby's eyebrows were as thick as her hair, nearly meeting above an ample nose. Catherine could imagine hairy masses of curls under her arms and dark hairs down her short legs. Catherine's stomach lurched and she vomited her supper of soup and sorrow into the mud.

Why couldn't Anton have fallen in love with a blonde, elegant model? Why did he have to pick a mole of a woman, a midget better fit to inhabit spaces under bridges, frightening tolls out of scared boys? That no-neck gnome had taken her man away. Horrible to be jealous of an ugly dwarf. It was demeaning.

The love scales fell from Catherine's eyes and the form she carried in her head of Anton's reverted into a shanky, slack-mouthed slip of a man. Her muscular teddy bear diminished to a slovenly weakling.

The mold smell of her first dream, when Mont Saint Michel swallowed the world, returned to her nostrils. Shelby probably smelled like that, musk perfume and harsh soap combined into the earthy fragrance.

Catherine shook her head. Maybe the mud on her own hands and hair carried the smell. How could she get to her room without being seen? It must be late because some of the floodlights around the Mont were being turned off.

Tourists often washed their feet in the Avancèe Outpost drinking fountain inside the main gate. It would have to do. She trudged back.

Not only was she an idiot, now she was a filthy idiot. Where had she first gone wrong? She tried to backtrack from the moment she saw Shelby's dress. Even then, she hoped Shelby was marrying anyone but Anton. Nuns married Christ, didn't they? The girl was in a convent.

Catherine wondered what her own IQ was. Mother had bragged about it without really telling her. Upper two percent. How could a genius be an emotional midget? She was too retarded to recognize a hotel manager's manners did not equate undying love. She needed help!

And, Anton had seen her unbutton her blouse and she'd thrown herself on his desk. Any mongrel could have figured out a man does not kiss the woman he loves on the forehead. She had been purposefully blind. She hadn't wanted to question anything. How could she secure her place on Mont Saint Michel, if Anton didn't love her?

She looked up at Saint Michael, maybe for the last time. She wished she'd kept her mother ignorant of the nude sketch. Now she would have to explain about the dress.

But, Mother knew. Mrs. Bermont and she had gone up to see the dress and Mother had been too embarrassed to tell her. But Catherine wished she had. What if Anton hadn't been such a prince?

Saint Michael's statue still shone, reaching toward the darkened silent heavens.

Mother had said, "The Mont is imagination and reality fused together."

Catherine kidded her, "Piling up stones dug out of the bay mud seems a low form of praise to the Lord."

Reality had trampled out all her dreams. Catherine gazed up at the empty platform space, which faced the west entrance to the Abbey. A rosy glow from her imagination or a late beam from the setting sun illuminated a cloud over the terrace. She judged the imagined Dome's balance with the peaked side of the Merveille.

A bubble of hope sprang away from her heart, but Catherine did not reach to reclaim the dream.

When she got to the main gate, no one watched as the village idiot put her head under the drinking fountain to rinse out most of the mud. Some of the muck had already hardened and flaked off like plaster. She took off her shoes and socks and washed them. Her jeans would have to be thrown away.

Catherine wrung the water out of her thick shock of hair. She could feel warmth under her feet from the sunbaked cobblestones, but she was beginning to shake from the damp. The cold water from the fountain had not helped. Shame kept a firm grip on her mind.

Two English mortars sat in the courtyard in front of the second gate called the Boulevard Gate. Catherine patted them as she passed by. She had tried to conquer the Mont too. Her onslaught had been about as effective as the English attempt.

She passed the Hotel Poulard and entered the King's Gate over its small drawbridge. The Artichoke house reminded her of the first entrance she had made to the Mont. Catherine thought she should have taken the prisoner's warning more to heart. Mont Saint Michel was certainly a terrible place to fall in love.

Catherine dripped down to the hotel, up the dark hotel stairs to her room, and took off her jeans while she stood in the shower stall. She dropped them on a towel on the floor. The shampoo took some of the swampy smell out of her hair.

Finally, when all the hot water was gone and the mud had washed down the drain, Catherine stepped out and rolled her hair up into a towel.

She found a warm jogging outfit and clean socks.

Grabbing her brush and comb, she sat down in front of the pedestal mirror to brush out her long hair. Her hair resisted her attempts to untangle it with the brush. For years, she had patiently played with it. Catherine looked at her stupid face in the standing mirror, her vain hair.

The first day Anton had touched the ends of her hair, she had been on top of the world believing he was attracted to her. Her scalp hurt when she pulled the knots out of her hair with the comb. Her arms ached from working at the chore. She should have cut the red strands off and nailed them to a stick for him to sketch. Was that only five days ago?

Catherine started to cry again, but she persisted and finally was able to plait the drying hair into one long braid. She tied her green scarf around the braid to keep the strands in place in bed. The scarf re-triggered her grief.

She had imagined Anton pulling at the silk scarf when they had supper with Mrs. Bermont. And then leaning his head down into her hair, saying he needed a fresh fragrance. All make-believe, but she thought Anton meant for her to stay forever in his mother's house. Well he could have the dreary place.

Catherine rummaged through her mother's room looking for scissors. First, she found the flashlight she had needed earlier, then the mending shears. She tore off the scarf, pulled her braid over her shoulder, and hacked it off.

There. She was free of him!

She laid the braid in her lap and looked at herself in the oval mirror. Her knees were weak from the spent anger. She brushed out the remaining hair. It was lopsided and jagged. Her neck was too long. She looked like a frightened scarecrow.

Perhaps she could tell Mother that Joan of Arc demanded she imitate her short hair. Mother would not buy the lie and would only worry about her sanity. Her patient mother had rolled the long tresses into different styles. Gentle she was when Catherine wanted to try some new strengthening or oil treatment.

Mother loved her hair. Catherine often caught her admiring it, especially when the sunlight seemed to cast a halo off its strawberry brightness. The mother swan loved the ugly duckling. Mother adored her, even without the camouflage of hair.

Catherine hadn't thought of her mother when she sawed off the wet hunks of braid. It was too late now. She would have to own up to the disaster.

Would Anton be in trouble with his family once they found out she'd cut her hair? She would not be able to hide under the tent of her own hair anymore. Her actions had bared her soul and her head. Poor Anton, he was innocent and now they might think he had led her on. And what would his fiancée think when she heard the story? It was all Catherine's fault.

The next time she did anything, she would have to think of it as a chess move, weighing the implications to the other pieces on the board. Catherine felt a painful widening of her self-indulgent heart and then a certain relief. She was now a part of the rest of bungling humanity. No longer a goddess descending from her ivory tower, she was down in the dirt with the rest of them.

Catherine laid the shorn braid carefully on the floor under the pedestal of the mirror. She grabbed the white bedspread and draped it over her head. Where was Mother? If she didn't die, Mother would kill her.

And where was Joan of Arc? Sure stop her on the steps of the greenhouse, right at the point when she would find out about the wedding dress, and *not* give her even a hint her whole life was going down some stinking drain. St. Joan had her nerve, asking for a replica of the greenhouse to commemorate what she'd accomplished for France. Catherine thought even a whisper of caution would have helped. Well, this was it. Life would never get any worse.

"St. Joan, go and get Mother," Catherine ordered.

She lit a candle at the base of the mirror and leaned back. Her outline wavered in the candlelight, which shifted the reflections until Catherine saw Mrs. Bermont and Mother standing outside of a florist shop in Paris. In the mirror, the lights inside the shop glowed on her mother's face.

She hardly recognized Anton's mother. Her short pink opera dress testified that Mrs. Bermont had given up wearing black mourning clothes.

Catherine could hear her mother's voice, "I thought a flower stall meant a cart on the street, not this gigantic nursery."

"Bernie's husband, my brother, builds ships for a living," Gail explained. "She's been teaching me how to run the flower business, sort of a correspondence course on management. The hardest thing to learn is which questions to ask the accountant."

In the mirrored vision Mother and Mrs. Bermont entered the shop and Mother was introduced to the owner, Bernice Laurent. Mrs. Laurent called her son to come out from a back workplace.

Catherine sat up straight in her chair on the Mont. Introductions were made to Mrs. Laurent's doe-eyed son, Romèe.

"My Romèe," Catherine said.

This was better than television.

In the mirror, Romèe looked around as if he had just heard his name called. Catherine thanked St. Joan with her whole heart for the answer to her prayers. Then she threw herself on the bed covering her shorn head with the covers. Prone, her failures washed over her like a tide of nails.

How could she make it in the real world, in college? These silly drawings, drainage lines, cable trays, pump houses. Who was she kidding? Sure, a diamond mounted on the Mont had been cute, but who would pay a slip of a girl to design the silly thing. She would end up in some dowdy drafting job, repeating the same sewage lines again and again, accepting the fact no one expected anything from her, doing what she was told, thankful for her paycheck, eating, dying.

Catherine wished she were dead.

Wanting to stay on this stinking Mont was her first error. Believing a princess in a castle could find love, had been an infant's dream. She had no right to claim any place, especially in Anton's life just to stay on Mont Saint Michel.

She had ruined everything. Her hair was such a wreck that she probably couldn't even attend Mother's wedding. She was probably the youngest failure in history. Her enchanted passion for Mont Saint Michel had set the stage for her comeuppance, left her unsure of her next breath. Yet each sound did follow the one before, as surely as the clock now chimed midnight.

Time would let her catch up with this new imperfect thing she had fallen into, this girl whose future held work and determination, this woman who could still accomplish worthwhile structures of resounding value, a future architect of civilization, a builder of dreams.

She could design buildings with spaces where people would feel at home with themselves. The windows would be angled or rounded. No one need feel imprisoned in a rat-cage shoebox looking out on a world of blank walls and parking lots full of abandoned cars and overflowing garbage bins.

Every dining room would have a flower terrace, even on the twentieth floor. Every bedroom would contain a continuous fountain spilling down a sloping wall just outside its window. Each circular front room would sport a glowing gas fire at its center to provoke family stories. Only the dark den and the kitchen would allow television cables for movies, news, gossip, or recipes. Wondering how she could incorporate a filter into her waterfall projects, Catherine finally closed down to sleep.

Friday, June 7th

Mother was crying when she woke Catherine the next morning. She held Mother's hands, as she had each time widowhood descended on her mother. Two or three more rings graced Mother's fingers now.

Ten, Catherine remembered she had been only ten when her father, Simon Marksteiner, had died; fourteen when Mother had thrown George out; and seventeen when Jimmy had had his first stroke.

Mother's grief-stricken stance, hunched in upon herself with a streaming red face responded to Catherine's method of comfort. Her choking sobs slowly subsided with each stroke of her daughter's hand.

Shocked at the papery thin fabric of her mother's skin, Faint, lined maps were waiting for the wrinkles to appear. The scene of their shared grief was so familiar, Catherine finally asked, "Who died?"

"Your hair!" Mother moaned.

Catherine joined her mother in heart-wrenching weeping.

"Shelby!" They sobbed together, naming the cause of the shorn locks.

"I felt like dying." Catherine pulled at her short hair. She coughed out St. Joan's story, between sobs. "I dreamt all night about Joan of Arc. She did visit here, according to the dream. No cannons. She paid for a pilgrim's pass, but the English got her when she left."

Mother put her arm around her fragile daughter. "St. Joan tried to escape against her Voices' advice."

"At the tower of Beau Revoir when she jumped." Catherine continued to weep quietly. "I don't want to die, still a virgin."

When they both had settled down and the tears had emptied out, Mother asked, "How did you find out about Shelby?" Catherine could only shake her head; her emotions were too close to the surface to speak. She finally gestured for her mother to answer first.

"Yesterday, before going to Paris," Mother said. "The size of the seed-pearl wedding dress let me know you weren't the intended. Mrs. Bermont promised Anton knew nothing about the dress. I thought I would have time to tell you about Shelby when I got back."

Mother stood up and pulled Catherine's legs free of the blankets. "Now, we have to hurry. Danny is meeting us for lunch at the Poulard Hotel. We have to pack. They'll move our belongings there as soon as you're ready."

Mother maneuvered Catherine into the shower. "Slick back your hair after you shampoo."

Catherine explained the bloody details into the shower's echo chamber. "I forced him to invite me to dinner."

Mother stuck her head in the shower. "Anton is donating his fish soup to the Poulard to feed our party."

"That's a lot of soup for three people.

She tried to come clean about throwing herself at Anton. "He showed me a picture of Shelby as a convent girl."

"Talk louder, dear," Mother called. "We have to be packed in time to return to Paris after lunch."

Almost yelling, Catherine repeated, "I threw myself at him."

"What?" her mother shouted back before coming into the bathroom. "Tell me again."

Catherine couldn't repeat the humbling words. She hung her head as she dripped out of the shower.

Mother dried her short locks. "Did Joan of Arc have anything to do with you cutting your hair?" Catherine shook her head. Mother directed her to dress quickly. "We're invited to Anton's wedding at sunset tomorrow. We have to shop in Paris for something to wear. We'll meet Shelby in Paris."

As Catherine dressed, her mother brought in her packed suitcases and dragged out Catherine's travel bags from under the bed. It was easier to talk when her mother was only half-listening. "I misunderstood Anton's trip into the bedroom and unbuttoned my blouse."

Mother stopped packing and touched Catherine's arm. "I know you meant to marry him, but I didn't understand why. You didn't know enough about him to love him."

"To stay on the Mont. Anton fled up to the roof just to get away from me."

"What?" her mother asked again.

Piqued by what appeared to be her mother's disinterest, Catherine's volume rose with each word. "Repeat what I've told you so far ....of the Major Tragedy of My LIFE!"

Mother sat down, directing Catherine to finish the packing. "Anton led you on by asking you to pose nude."

"Even after I saw the wedding dress, I wanted to believe Shelby might need it to marry Christ at the convent."

Mother busily checked all the drawers and set their suitcases out in the hall with Catherine's sketchpads between them.

"Do we have to leave because I cut my hair?"

"Of course not. Shelby will move in here tonight, and Danny is coming to the wedding, so the Bermonts have made reservations for us at the Poulard Hotel down the street."

"I have to meet Shelby." Catherine let her fingers touch the damp ends of her hair. She dragged her feet out of the room and staggered down the inner, narrow hotel steps. "I've ruined your wedding by lopping off my hair."

"Getting the ends trimmed and shaped will easily save the wedding." Her mother smiled. "How do you feel about Anton, now?"

Catherine had brushed her teeth, but a sour taste rose from her stomach. "I cut my braid off to give to Anton. My hair was the only thing he seemed to admire."

Mother stopped, dropping her large purse as she had the pink suitcase on the first day they climbed the path to the Bermont Hotel. Her mother ran back up the hotel steps and retrieved the braid from the floor beneath the pedestal mirror. She slipped it into her purse to take the beauty parlor.

Catherine stood in the street before the Hotel de Bermont. "I thought this was my future home," she said, staring up at the blue shuttered Inn.

Mother hustled her off to Mont Saint Michel's only beauty parlor. The second-story shop made use of mirrors to reflect its scant view of the bay. Rounded vanities with angled mirrors confused the patrons when they stepped down into the various stations. The perfumes of soaps, shampoos, and beauty creams assailed their nostrils. Beatles music further bewildered the air.

Mother sat next to Catherine's chair at an adjoining stanchion, then took Catherine's long strawberry blonde braid out of her bag and stroked it like a favorite cat.

The hairdresser's name was Delia. She had thick blonde hair down to her knees. She resembled a modernized Mary Magdalen. "I can make a beautiful wig out of your braid."

"My daughter's handiwork was caused over a lost love, whose wedding she has to attend tomorrow evening."

"Eighteen years of beautiful growth, now shorn," Delia said. "But, I can prepare a stunning hair-piece for you by five tomorrow."

Catherine ran her fingers over her itching scalp. Her grief wasn't just for the loss of her hair. Her scalp tickled from embarrassment. "Have I ever been attractive?" "Maybe people only stared at my hair without even seeing me."

Delia swiveled the chair, so Catherine's back was to the mirror.

Catherine reached out a hand for her mother. "Aren't you disappointed in me?"

"The hair will grow," Mother said.

"Youth is your only flaw," Delia said. "Inexperience."

When Catherine was placed under the hairdryer, the proprietress offered them a fragrant green tea. "I don't believe in coffee. It clogs the sinuses, blocks the bowels and is addictive. Let coffee sit in a cup for a day and see if I'm lying. Cement it is."

"I think tea is probably just as destructive as coffee," Mother said.

Catherine accepted her warm mug. "I can't help staring at the statues of Saint Theresa and Saint Frances in your window display."

"Pick up the St. Theresa," Delia said.

When Catherine squeezed the rubber doll, it sounded like a dog's squeaky toy. Catherine laughed out loud; but when she replaced the doll, her eyes overflowed with tears.

Delia took her hand. "Go ahead and cry. I can make the wig with a central part or make a straight pulled-back crown."

Catherine said, "I don't care."

Delia asked, "Is that a passive-aggressive remark? Choose."

Mother scowled at Delia. "Who gave you permission to bully my daughter?" Unruffled, Delia said, "Sometimes the injured need to take a first step. Making a decision is like a baby's first step." Catherine decided on the straight back look. Delia agreed with her choice.

"I usually consider that hairdressers are medicine women," Mother said as Delia finished snipping hair at the base of Catherine's neck.

Delia spun Catherine around to face the mirror, spreading her hands over Catherine's head. "Behold the magic."

Catherine's new pixie cut showed off her delicate ears and emphasized her great green eyes. Mother agreed the cut was beautifully done.

"A good hair style is better for a body than any drug," Delia said.

Catherine said. "I'm relaxed."

But Delia wasn't convinced. She shook her head. "Look at your hands."

Mother unfolded Catherine's fists. Catherine stifled a sob, "I will never be okay for lunch."

Delia said, "I have the perfect mantra. I guarantee you will be able to smile all through lunch with a heart at peace. It was J. C.'s favorite." Mother and Catherine gave her questioning look. "Jesus Christ. It was the only prayer He said anyone ever needed to say."

While they repeated the prayer aloud, in unison, Catherine could feel peace descending on her soul. "Our Father, who art in heaven, hallowed be Thy Name. Thy Kingdom come, Thy will be done on earth as it is in Heaven." A surge of warm energy from on high flowed through Catherine, to the very bottom of her feet. "Give us this day our daily bread...," Catherine admitted, she was getting hungry. "...and forgive us our trespasses as we forgive those who trespass against us." That seemed fair. "Lead us not into temptation..." Never again. "...but deliver us from evil." No sense using energy to try to get even. "...for Thine is the Kingdom, and the Power, and the Glory forever and ever. Amen."

Mother gave Delia a $100 tip.

Delia accepted the money. "I'm happy you value the gifts the Lord has given me."

CHAPTER TWELVE

Outside the beauty salon Catherine and Mother met Anton and Romèe carrying their bags to the Hotel Poulard. Catherine no longer saw any resemblance between the cousins. Romèe's dark thick curls formed ringlets at the nape of his neck, at the corners of his brow, and just above his ears. The cut softened Romèe's cheek bones, square jaw, cleft chin and prominent nose. His mouth was smaller than Anton's, almost puckish.

Wearing Docker slacks with a light blue pullover, he rolled about like a drunken sailor. And Romèe had magnificent eyes, the black sheen of the iris accentuated the pupils as they darted about until fixing on Catherine. His gaze became arrow points of attention. "I'm baaack," Romèe drawled, mimicking one of cinemas' ghostly terrors.

He clasped Catherine's hands in his. She looked down at their hands to avoid his eyes. His hands were oversized even for his coltish height, as if he were a young pup, growing into his paws.

Catherine glanced up and gave him an open smile. He was more attractive now. In the glimpse she had received via St. Joan in the mirror the night before, he looked sweet; but then she hadn't felt the comforting warmth of his touch.

Anton stepped forward. "Your new hairstyle enhances your beauty. You know, at times, you made Romèe feel invisible."

"Once, in a mirage, I think." Catherine stammered.

Lunch was a lavish affair in a private dining room of the Poulard Hotel. Morning glories were blooming at the windows. The tall windows had been cranked open slightly and the weedy vines spread blue triumphant horns into every available air space like some mad gardener's dream.

Romèe wrapped his arm around Catherine's. "Sit with me."

Was she being pitied because of Shelby? "I won't be able to eat unless you let go."

"Isn't he a beauty?" Mother whispered too loudly and everyone laughed.

But Romèe said in a serious tone, making everyone else disappear from the table. "Your mother tells me you have drawn an exquisite, glass addition for the Abbey's ruined west nave."

"I'll show you my sketches." It was an effort to draw her eyes away from his approving face. His admiration healed her wounded pride.

"I'm going back to Paris with you to meet Shelby," Romèe said. "When we return to the Mont tonight, we will make time to examine your work." Romèe continued to hold Catherine's hand and placed it in her lap, as he smiled.

Catherine could feel her body struggling not to respond. She didn't mean to let her stupid heart get hurt again on a rebound.

As they were being served Anton's soup, Danny Passantino arrived.

Catherine caught her mother's chair from falling, as Mother jumped up to embrace him.

Danny's white hair emphasized his olive complexion and Italian good looks. After introductions were made, Catherine tugged her mother's elbow to wrestle her attention away from Danny. "I asked St. Joan to get you in Paris, after I cut my hair."

Romèe stopped eating to stare.

Mother crossed herself.

Catherine explained, "St. Joan provided a vision of the Paris flower shop in my mirror. I saw you, Mother, Mrs. Bermont, Mrs. Laurent, and this man staring at me now. It was better than television. I could hear you, and Romèe listened when I called his name."

"I did hear you," Romèe said.

"You've been blessed with the gift," Danny Passantino said, cuddling his future, step-daughter's cropped head before he took his seat next to Mother.

Catherine dominated the conversation. "I had another dream, too. Joan of Arc did come to Mont Saint Michel before she was captured."

"I think I dreamt the same dream," Romèe said. "The winds were whipping around. It must have been winter."

Catherine nodded to Romèe. "There were Scotsmen that St. Joan knew."

"They were eating before a big fire in the Knights Hall," Romèe told the group, "with maps spread out under their bowls of stew."

Catherine questioned Romèe, "Didn't you tell me St. Joan never came to Mont Saint Michel

"That was me," Anton said. "No material proof."

Mother said, "The four months before Joan of Arc's trial were not accounted for. Andrew Lang said he found no record of her whereabouts from January through April of the year she died. The Dauphin lived on borrowed money from Scotland even after he was crowned. Scotland also had joined the fight against the English at the Mont. Was she in armor this time?"

"I know it sounds crazy," Catherine said. "She wore a gold T-shirt under a long fur coat or robe. At first, I thought her hair had grown long, but it was her fur collar turned up against the cold draft in the hall. She wasn't very pretty, Mother. Wasn't she supposed to be tall?"

"Some historians say so," Mother told the five other luncheon guests, "while others maintain she had a short, stocky build.

I liked her voice," Catherine said; "Even though I didn't understand her words. St. Joan was excited about something. The Scots were promising her things while she nodded."

"Were you in the hall too?" Romèe asked.

"Yes," Catherine said. "I was toward the ceiling. I had even longer hair and it floated around the hem of my blue nightgown. The other people in the Knights Hall couldn't see me."

Romèe could not stop watching Catherine. Why had her mother let her cut her gorgeous hair? It was true, she was even more striking. Her innocent green eyes held a hint of sensual sparkle.

Aunt Gail explained for Danny, "St. Joan's army refused to utter an oath of any kind after she convinced them the Lord wouldn't help the French if they took His name in vain."

"What did you dream about?" Catherine asked Romèe.

Romèe coughed. "Kind of silly stuff, but in the movie, I mean dream, Joan was showing me flowers, saying their names. Her hair was short too." Romèe wanted to cut out his tongue. Why did he mention short hair?

Catherine blushed deeply and looked over at Anton.

Aunt Gail came to his rescue. "You have the key, Romèe. Catherine might want to see the inside of the Artichoke house before we go off to Paris."

Catherine stood up immediately, and her mother smiled. Romèe meant to finish his omelet but laid down his fork. "It's just next door, a minute away."

St. Joan stepped through the fragrant portal that the morning glories provided from the near world. "I could swear."

Brother Richard let go of her sleeve. "I wish you would just warn me when you intend to invade this rough world."

"He missed my entire point of dreaming to him," St. Joan said stomping her laced boot.

"Romèe remembered the flowers." Brother Richard stuck his ghostly finger into the chocolate frosting of one donut in a pile of them in the center of the table.

"Stop that," St. Joan commanded. "You can't taste anything anyway."

"But I remember," Brother Richard said, rolling his eyes heavenward from the recalled taste of chocolate, "You can contact him when his mind is less taken up with his first love."

"All these hormones are so annoying." St. Joan tugged on Brother Richard's rope belt to take him away from the table and back through the morning glory gate to their side of the world.

Romèe and Catherine's steps echoed in the entrance way of the Artichoke House. "Slate," Romèe said, meaning the tile.

Catherine roamed quickly through the bare rooms, taking in the view from each window. "No one can see in the windows, so you needn't bother with drapes." Then she was off to the kitchen, opening cupboard doors. "I love a small kitchen," she called out, as Romèe joined her.

The light from the window above the sink bounced off the copper pots hanging over the stove and created an aura above Catherine's glistening red hair. Romèe pointed, awestruck, "Don't move," he said, "a halo."

"I cut off my hair to give to Anton," she said, pulling on the shortened pieces, "after he told me about Shelby."

Romèe felt the shock of his continuing anger against Anton return. He wanted to hit something, so he struck the pot nearest him. The pan knocked into the next one, which continued the force to three others, producing a cacophony of sound.

Catherine laughed and held her ears.

Romèe tried to quiet the unruly pots. "Anton told me you were great about Shelby's dress."

Catherine put her hand on his shoulder. "He did?"

"But you weren't okay?" Romèe secured her hand on his shoulder with his own.

"I went for a walk and fell down in the mud," Catherine pulled away. "My hair was full of the muck. I washed and braided it, before I hacked it off. Anton only liked my hair."

"Catherine," was all Romèe could muster, as he pulled her to his chest. "I've loved you since you set foot on Mont Saint Michel. I leased this place so you would understand my intentions are serious."

Catherine turned her face up to his, and closed her eyes.

He kissed her soft lips. They were warm and sweet. He wanted to devour her on the spot. His boiling blood threatened.

She stepped away from him. "I don't want to hurt you if I'm on a rebound...from a fantasy affection."

"Any girl would be have been seduced by the attention Anton gave you," Romèe said, not wanting to mention nudity or the sketch.

"I don't want to talk about him." Catherine turned back to opening drawers in the kitchen. "I've made such a fool of myself."

"Did you see the fireplace's swinging arm?" Romèe asked, consenting to keep the conversation away from her injury. "We can fix popcorn at night."

"You can," Catherine corrected. "I have to return to school."

"Do you have to go back with your mother? I'd like to take you on a tour of the continent...to get your mind off things."

Catherine stood on the brick rim of the fireplace as she reached up to the mantle. "I can hardly touch the shelf."

Out of control, Romèe grabbed her around the waist, spinning her out into the room. "I loved it when you twirled around on the Abbey terrace."

Catherine stroked the back of her neck. "It will grow."

"Yes, yes." Romèe felt like an imbecile to bring her hair up again. "Come see the terrace."

Off the paneled living room, a pair of stained-glass panel doors led to the patio. The Mont's brick walkway surrounded the garden, which was filled with the fragrances of white lilies and red roses.

Once outside, they could hear the restaurant chatter next door filtering over the wall.

Standing on a convenient stone bench, Catherine peaked over the enclosure. She motioned for Romèe to station himself next to her.

There she was in his garden! He wanted to fall down and hug her knees. He loved her from the roots of his hair down to the soles of his feet.

She waved again, more insistently; but shushing him.

As he looked over the wall he saw Danny Passantino and her mother holding hands, not speaking, just staring into each other's eyes.

Without thinking he said, loud enough for them to hear. "I love you, Catherine."

Catherine jumped down from her perch.

Before joining her, Romèe noticed her mother laughed and waved at him. Now all he had to do was convince this imp of a girl he meant his declaration of affection. "Come travel on the continent with me for a week."

"I'll think about it," she said, taking his hand. "Let's see the rest of your house, Citizen Laurent."

CHAPTER THIRTEEN

Saturday, June 8th

Romèe was relieved because Anton could *not* go to Paris on Saturday. Shelby's wedding arrangements required Anton remain on the Mont. Catherine's contact with Anton would have been a strain. And, Romèe hoped she would pay some attention to him. In fact, he never wanted to let her out of his sight again. Look what had happened to her hair after leaving her alone for one night.

Before boarding the bus from Mont Saint Michel to Avranches, Romèe asked Mrs. Marksteiner to sit up front with Danny and Aunt Gail. Despite his obvious ploy, Mrs. Marksteiner kept checking on Romèe and Catherine.

Mrs. Marksteiner concealed her chaperone duties by taking pictures of the retreating outline of Mont Saint Michel.

The bus arrived fifteen minutes early for the train. At the station, Mrs. Marksteiner, Danny and Aunt Gail talked non-stop to Catherine. She appeared more self-conscious than when Romèe first spied her getting off the tourist bus, less than a week earlier. Her motions lacked the lighthearted panache of the girl Romèe had let into his heart.

A certain dignity or awareness of inner strength tied strings to Catherine's shoulders, letting her walk with a statelier gait, as if the goddess revealed herself for the first time. Catherine continued to tread gracefully into the chambers of Romèe's inner world.

Behind the backs of the group, Romèe circled like an orphaned puppy. He sauntered up and down the short train-station platform, marking off

126

steps of increasing boredom. The sight of the oncoming train relieved him of further negative ruminations.

Once on the train, the older women and Danny sat about four seats ahead of Romèe and Catherine. They were chatting about their own weddings long ago, Mrs. Marksteiner's upcoming wedding with Danny, and the clothes they planned for Shelby and where Anton should honeymoon.

Catherine must have felt like a wet blanket on the festive conversations. Romèe tried to make upbeat, polite comments about the scenery to take her mind off whatever detail of her recent humiliation she was mulling over. Catherine didn't need his pity, but he hoped she found comfort in his hand holding onto hers.

The clanking of the train wheels seemed to saw at her nerves. If they didn't get to Paris soon, Romèe felt Catherine might strangle him, or start a scream she couldn't finish.

A black wall seemed to rise between them, denying any access. Catherine's imprisoned frustrations emanated in steady waves from her. The seats were hard. Directly in front of them an unshaven, old man's clothing smelled of moth-balls. Catherine was angry at the whole world and the train's aromas were not helping. The sun was too bright too, because Catherine put on her sunglasses, hiding her gorgeous green eyes. The train rocked too much. Her elbow banged into the armrest. Romèe offered his blue sweater as a cushion under her arm.

Then, a badly dressed girl about Catherine's age decided to have a cigarette. She stood behind them in the passageway between the cars. The door to their section opened allowing the smoke and a cold draft to reach them.

Catherine put on Romèe's sweater and waved the smoke away, before it dawned on Romèe to get up and shut the door. Catherine rummaged for something in her purse, then handed Romèe a breath mint.

'Oh, no. My breath's bad.' Dejectedly Romèe thanked Catherine and started watching passengers board the train at each of the irritating stops.

As if to ameliorate the slight insult of offering him a breath mint, Catherine said, "I like your hair."

Romèe promptly imagined Catherine holding on to the back of his neck as she had at their first kiss. Catherine removed her sunglasses and

Romèe caught her staring at him. He could feel an embarrassing blush flood his cheeks. She nervously pulled at her own shortened hair.

"I don't think that will make it grow any faster," he whispered.

Mrs. Marksteiner and her fiancé, Danny Passantino, laughed at something Aunt Gail said probably unrelated to Catherine. However, Catherine's emotional turmoil sent a tear sliding down her cheek. She tried to cough and find a tissue in her purse to wipe her nose. Romèe insisted she use his handkerchief.

"I like my hair short," Catherine lied.

"You look very chic."

She made an effort to smile. "A young woman's hair is a tribute to her mother's diligence. I'll be on my own in a month and I can manage better with my hair shorter."

"I liked the flow of your hair when the tresses hung down to your knees."

"When I braided it, it only came to my waist." Romèe knew she was sorry for chopping off her hair. Anton was the cause. "When I cut my hair, it was still in a braid," she said. "I kept the braid." She patted his knee casually. "Delia, the hairdresser, is going to make me wig."

There was nothing nonchalant about his reaction to her touch. He wanted to take her in his arms right there in front of everyone. He wanted to wipe away, erase every injury. Instead, Romèe covered her hand with his and smiled.

Catherine accepted his touch. She smiled in return. "When we get back to Mont Saint Michel tonight, I'll show you my drawings of St. Joan's Dome. We will have time to look at the photographs you took of my hair flowing over the wall of the Abbey's bell tower. I resemble Rapunzel in the fairy tale."

"Rapunzel?" Romèe asked. "Do you mean Rumpelstiltskin?"

"No," Catherine laughed for the second time that day.

Mrs. Marksteiner looked back at them; and Romèe read relief on her face.

"Rumpelstiltskin," Catherine said, "stamped himself into the ground from anger when the princess found out his name. Rapunzel is the girl with long hair that she let down from a tower for her lover to climb up and rescue her."

Suddenly, Catherine seemed to turn away in disgust.

Romèe said, "Don't you want to dig your nails into some man's arm or beat your fists on my chest? Pull my stupid hair out by the roots?"

"I'll never see St. Joan's Dome built anyway." Catherine let herself sink lower in the seat.

"You could rip up my shirt and shove it down Anton's throat."

"Or your throat," Catherine said, "to stop your dulcet, intoxicating male tones. Let the whole world die." After a short time, peace returned. "I'm sorry, I'm such a grump."

"You've had a shock. Anton's talents don't provide awareness of the emotional world around him. When he focuses on a problem, he can solve it. Most of the time he's not even conscious of his words."

"I fit that description," Catherine said. "I can't fathom a world beyond my own perceptions. I wish people would hang signs on things: 'Here's reality,' or 'That's a dream.' I need help distinguishing my own imaginings from real life."

Romèe had to look across the aisle away from her, as he muttered, "Asking a young virgin to pose nude is unforgivable."

Catherine was silent for a moment. "Thanks for championing my idiotic infatuation with Anton." She squeezed his hand. "Virgins aren't always irrepressible."

"Anton's a man of integrity, but he was wrong to encourage you."

Then Romèe spoke of another virgin, "Joan of Arc won Mark Twain's homage. I remember reading: 'A rich world made empty and poor (by her death). She was built on a grander scale than the mass of mankind, moved on a loftier plane. The only entirely unselfish person whose name has a place in profane history.'"

Catherine rested her head against Romèe's shoulder. Romèe leaned forward not to miss a word, and to smell her hair. She said, "I think St. Joan drew the Dome to epitomize her hopes for France."

Romèe locked his arms around Catherine. 'Please, Lord,' he prayed silently, 'let me keep her safe from now on.'

Aloud Romèe said, "I bet Joan of Arc felt alone when she was betrayed into English hands and tried in the Church Court as a heretic, sorceress and blasphemer."

Joan of Arc appeared in the aisle of the train.

Catherine stirred slightly; but Romèe heard St. Joan whisper, "I've been called a mad chambermaid, a beggar's brat, enchantress, orgayne of the devil; even that I repudiated my father."

Romèe said aloud to Catherine and St. Joan, "In 1611 in the <u>History of Great Britain</u>, John Speed mentions St. Joan the paragon as, 'uttering nothing more than that which was modest, chaste and holy with a modest countenance sweet, civil and resolute'."

"Captivating qualities," Catherine commented.

Romèe felt a tremor in the immense oceans of the universe. "In my dream," he looked directly at his vision of St. Joan, "St. Joan's complexion's dark, her wide-set eyes fit for the face of a Saint."

Catherine added, "St. Joan's personality must have been impossible to resist. I read in the trial's transcript St. Joan told her judges it was the will of God to do what He puts into your mind." Close to Romèe's left ear, Catherine said, "She created her own miracles."

St. Joan whispered into his right, "I created faith in the possible."

Catherine asked him, "Do you believe in a central originating force, something akin to a pure mathematician?"

"I know I cannot understand the Lord's affection for me."

"Attention turns away," Catherine said. "Affection stays."

"We are beloved of the Lord."

"God in our pockets," Catherine sighed. Romèe couldn't tell if the sigh was from resignation or satisfaction. Catherine said almost to herself, "I wonder if all virgins are in a rush to be otherwise?"

Romèe laughed. "St. Joan would have laid siege to the clouds."

"It's remarkable we both think so highly of St. Joan. I remember her words, 'Were they (the English) hanging from the clouds, we yet should drag them down.'"

Romèe said, "Well I'm a virgin. And I can tell you honestly if I lived for too long in the United States, I'd be trying to jump that line."

Catherine's mother called back to him, "You've been to the States?"

They both laughed and Romèe shook his head. "Yes, Madame, educated in Ann Arbor. I was only a visitor to the Mont—at my Aunt's hotel. But this week, I leased the Artichoke House for ninety-nine years. Now I am a citizen."

Before Romèe caught Catherine's eye, he saw her mother's sly smile.

In the Paris train station, Mother asked Catherine to help her find a bathroom. Danny and Mrs. Bermont had gone out front with Romèe to hail a taxi. Catherine used her bad French and the card she had written for such an emergency, but the ticket attendants only pointed up a stairway.

Mother and Catherine found something like a shower-stall drain in the floor, with two coin-operated doors at each side, but none of their coins worked. A man came up the stairs, slipped in the correct coin, entered the stall, and then left. Catherine tried to stop him to exchange their coins, but he brushed her aside.

"Don't let anyone up those stairs," Mother said. "I wasn't born on a farm for nothing."

As Catherine kept watch, she could hear her mother take care of business over the open drain. Catherine followed her example as Mother guarded the stairs. They giggled like school girls at their escapade when they joined their hosts outside. Unwilling to break up their twosome, Catherine and Mother convinced Romèe to ride in a cab with his aunt and Danny.

Catherine had forgotten her camera, but Mother lent hers when their taxi got caught in traffic. Catherine rolled down the window and snapped a picture of the Louvre's glass pyramid, climbed over Mother and shot the Arch of Triumph.

When they got out of the cab at the wedding dress shop on Blvd. De Magenta, next to Haut-Marais, Mother embarrassed Catherine with a bear hug. "I love you, trooper."

"I cheer her up, don't I?" Romèe said as he guided them to the sedate dress shop's viewing room.

"She cheers herself up," Mother said, but she patted Catherine's shoulder.

Shelby was waiting for them. She was a head shorter than Catherine, and her features were enhanced by a shock of black-brown hair. As they embraced, Shelby put her hand on Catherine's face. "Anton captured you well."

Catherine wished she hadn't cut her hair; she wanted Shelby to like her. Suddenly, she could hardly think of anything to say. "But you are his Shelby. Have you read Shelby's <u>The Constant Lover</u>?"

Shelby curtsied to her, "I have read it. It's the reason why Anton named me Shelby Constance."

Mrs. Bermont directed the dress traffic around them. Models in Shelby's size helped her pick out her trousseau. They sat in comfortable chairs, pointing to the clothes they wanted without actually going through the tiresome task of trying them on.

A light lunch was served, with plenty of chilled champagne. Danny and Romèe helped the women make a couple of decisions. To save luggage space, Mother sent most of the items home to the States, except for their wedding-guest dresses.

Mother and Danny began discussing Mrs. Bermont's new apartment in Paris.

Catherine remarked to Mrs. Bermont, "I don't see how you can leave your home on Mont Saint Michel."

Mrs. Bermont smiled at Shelby. "Because my son's wife will need a home of her own."

Shelby spoke quietly to Catherine, "Anton mentioned you never want to leave the Mont."

"I don't," Catherine said, surprised at the catch in her voice.

Romèe covered for her by asking, "Have you finished your sketches on St. Joan's addition to the Abbey?"

"I did." Catherine said. "I'll be able to present them to my graduate advisor in the fall."

"That will be months from now," Romèe said. "Do you have to return with your mother?"

"No, she doesn't," her mother said. "I have to get ready for my wedding, but Catherine could stay."

"Let me show you the rest of France before you go home. My father thinks we should make the grand tour through Italy and Spain." His father would be proud of him. He had finally invited her.

"It's just what you need," Mrs. Marksteiner agreed.

Catherine seemed surprised. "I would like to see Rouen, and Florence, and Madrid!"

"Absolutely!" Romèe said. "After Anton's wedding, we'll set off!"

"If I go, I'll need more clothes," Catherine said to the delight of everyone in the dress shop.

CHAPTER FOURTEEN

Avanches

T hat evening after a long formal rehearsal supper in Avranches, the party returned to Mont Saint Michel. Catherine and Romèe left Mother and Danny at a rampart cafe in the evening's fading light. Romèe suggested a walk around the outside of the Mont.

When Catherine looked back, Danny was holding his hand under Mother's chin speaking intently. Their noses were hardly six inches apart.

Catherine stepped through the last gateway, and turned to the right to circle the island counter-clockwise. She reminisced about her first entrance through the gate. How the courtyard stones had sucked out any of the sun's warmth, as if they could vacuum out the marrow of her bones. The Mont itself immediately possessed her.

"Maybe my infatuation with Anton was initiated by wanting to live on the Mont."

"Perhaps the Mont had the same idea."

"Or Joan of Arc." Catherine pursued the topic as they stood for a moment in Saint Aubert's chapel. "She awarded me with an inheritance, the drawings for St. Joan's Dome. They're too professional for a high school graduate to accomplish."

Catherine stopped talking for the rest of the walk. She enjoyed hearing Romèe talk on and on as they slogged through the wet sand around the Mont.

"In peaceful times a windmill was constructed over the chimneys of the Gabriel Tower," Romèe said. Then his parents were the focus of his soliloquy and the wealth they refused to let him mention in school. Romèe followed her quickened pace back to her new lodgings at the Poulard Hotel.

The roof slanted in gloomy room 105, which was filled with a double bed. The path to the windows was blocked with Catherine's suitcases. The new purchases were piled on top of the bags. It was a good thing the bathroom door had been left open. If Romèe had stretched out his arms, he would have jammed his fist through the wall.

"You couldn't swing a cat in here if you tried," he said.

Catherine pushed past him to test the view. A mishmash of back yard stonewalls climbed up a slight incline. Placed along their ledges were depressing pots of dead flowers.

Standing close behind her, Romèe shared the ugly view. "Your drawings?"

"There." Catherine pointed to the pile of sketch books wedged between the suitcases.

Romèe rescued them, as Catherine climbed onto the wall-to-wall bed. "Maybe we should take them to my Artichoke house."

Catherine patted the bed. "Lean against the headboard. Romèe tried, keeping his feet on the floor. Catherine flopped on her belly kicking off her sandals.

Romèe turned the pages of the sketchbook.

Catherine held her breath. Finally, she said, "The glass panels will be frosted a rose color. The watering and drainage lines can run up the triangular support beams."

"Where did you come up with the idea?"

Catherine laughed. "Actually, I was in a kind of daze, thinking I could watch Mother climb the Grand Staircase. When I woke up and looked at the sketch, the Dome was interlaced with these diamond-shaped supports." She turned the pages backward to the early glass pinnacle shapes mimicking the Merveille section of the Abbey. "These would be blown off by the first storm, but I think the Dome will survive. Memories attached themselves to the sight of some buildings."

"Noble lines earn the affection of masses of people," Romèe said. "You finished all of these in four days?"

"I couldn't seem to stop." Catherine said. "My mother agrees with my sanctification of place. Ghosts often seek particular addresses and refuse to leave until recognized." She couldn't shut up now. Nervousness kept the words flowing. "Maybe giving up doubt for certainty allows the brain to atrophy and people mistakenly name the deadness, inner peace."

"Driven," Romèe said, picking up the first sketch to look at the details again. "Wait a minute," Romèe's hands were in his hair again. "How many design classes did you have in college?"

"Three, if you count an art class." Catherine paced the floor between the bathroom door and the bed. "I think they're good, but I don't have the experience to judge them. They're too personal, important to me to weigh them professionally."

"You may be a genius. Where did you learn how girders are braced, how cable trays are laid, and the water pipes?" Romèe put one sketch against the door. "I'd like my father to see these. He knows architects in Paris. They could give you an unbiased opinion."

"I'd appreciate it." Catherine began collecting the sketches, placing each between clean sheets in the various sketching pads. "Is there anyway the architects could avoid knowing I'm not certified."

"I'm sure Father will think of a good ploy. Maybe we can run off blue prints under his construction buddy's logo."

"You could identify me as A. Marksteiner from Hungary."

"Hungarian princess," Romèe said, moving closer.

"It's funny," she said, "that you, the darker cousin, got lost in Anton's shadow." Catherine rested her palms on his chest. "How did that happen?"

"Bad luck," Romèe said, stretching her hands up to his neck and enclosing her in a tender embrace. He rubbed the back of her cropped head.

Catherine tipped her head back to look at him, and he tenderly kissed her mouth.

"I don't want to play around," Romèe said, as he held her.

"I don't want to let my heart go mad again." She struggled out of his arms and pranced around on top of the bed twirling with her arms out wide. Then Catherine stopped, surprised. "My hair created a private tent, but now it's gone. I want to see Mont Saint Michel at every sunset in every season. I won't miss the United States. Trees grow everywhere."

"We can start planting them in the marshes like the first forest the monks saw."

"You remember everything I've ever said?"

Romèe nodded. "We're all citizens of the earth."

"If enough people believed in Martians or extra-terrestrials as an external enemy, maybe we could get on with the economic and ecological renaissance of our world."

"You might miss the wide open spaces of the U.S.," Romèe said, "but the sea provides expansive views. I've envied Anton for years."

Catherine opened a suitcase filled with gifts for friends back home. The candles would serve a higher purpose here and she could buy more gifts in the airport shops. She arranged thirty-six of the glass shielded candles on a wide wainscoting ledge lining the walls. She positioned a double row on the windowsill with the smaller, vigil lights in front of the back row.

In their last song of the day, birds signaled it was time to recline. The place was looking good, as was Romèe who could talk an ear off a jaybird.

He was saying, "Anton knows people all over the world. I haven't told my parents, but I want to start a flower shop right here on Mont Saint Michel. There isn't one now and every wife is a sucker for flowers. We would probably see the same people every three years and be asked to visit them. Would you like that?"

She found the $950 bottle of red wine Mother had packed and succeeded in opening it. The bathroom glasses would have to do. She watched Romèe enjoy a glass and poured a refill for him.

"I think of you as a part of my life," he said. "Father taught me that learning a new language is a rehearsal for life. The personality first accumulates possessions (to have) before being able to identifying ourselves (to be). Once sure of whom we are and what we have to offer others, a young person wants something unique to accomplish (to do). We look around (to see) to find what needs doing. Usually we have to leave our parents (to go) to a new territory. Only then do we understand our place in the universe and the meaning to life. Then we know how to live. So in Italian: avere, essere, fare, andare, vedere, and sapere are the first verbs to learn: to have, to be, to do, to go, to see, to know how to. And 'fate' in Italian is the plural for 'you all do to me.' Not of our making, out of the control of our egos, that's fate. We have to leave it there, content to have, and be, and do, and go, and see, and learn how to live on our own.

The people around us are responsible for themselves. We unknowingly, innocently bump into other individuals' plans and change them."

It didn't matter what he said. Romèe's voice had claimed her.

Apparently, Catherine liked the sound of his voice. Even if flaws in his thinking included environmental issues, political intentions or undue monetary influences, she listened intently to the low resonance of his tones.

When Romèe escaped into the small shower room, his confidence slipped away. The word rebound played and replayed with the edges of his consciousness, then presented itself in Catherine's voice.

She sure liked candles, and that wine. Romèe wished he had the courage to open the door and ask for another glass. Why hadn't he told her about Anton's engagement? She might have retained her hair. As he opened the door, he caught a glimpse of himself in the bathroom mirror. He resembled a young boy about to leap to his death.

Catherine lay on the bed. Candlelight softened the shadows. Her short hair was fanned out on the pillow. Romèe knelt down, and Catherine played with his curls.

"I want you to love me," Romèe said. "Since you set foot on the Mont you owned my heart. Don't give up on me."

"St. Joan, herself will fish you up to heaven, "Catherine started blowing out the candles. Finally, the last candle was out and they sat in the dark. Nearly half-an-hour passed in silence.

Romèe stormed his brain to think of something to offer.

Catherine finally said. "I'm not sure I know how to face being alone."

"When you took the heaviest bags from your Mother when you got off the bus, I knew you were raised to be a loving person."

"I wanted to own the Mont," she said.

"Your body reacted with such delight to everything, like a new lamb."

"Even St. Joan told me to go to Romèe, the day you were gone."

"I didn't feel I was in competition with Anton. He was engaged," Romèe hoped Catherine would not say one word about Anton. He couldn't believe he brought up his name. The Imp of the Perverse Edgar Allen Poe wrote about controlled his tongue. "Terrible to be valued as part of a place."

"Terrible is this place," Catherine said.

Romèe hung his head and she scooted behind him, rubbing his back and hair, cooing to him. "I understand," she said. "You want to be sure I love you, too." As she bit the curls at the back of his neck, Catherine whispered, "I can feel my heart aching, like it's growing past the shell of my ribs. You are not just a boy I can claim on a whim. My self-indulgence is out of kilter. I want to prove myself to you. You are a man of integrity. I want you in my life."

He had not lost her!

Catherine gently put her hand in his open palm. "Some day when I touch you, you'll know with every nerve of your soul that, in truth, I belong to you."

Romèe couldn't ask for more, now. He flipped on the overhead light, and kissed her goodnight. "We'll take your drawings with us when we tour, and find a university to accept them as qualification for your entrance. We'll have time to get to know each other." Thankful, he was that he had not heard her mention rebound.

Sunday, June 9th

At the Hotel Poulard Catherine fluffed her pillow, spread her fingertips behind her head. Tomorrow, Monday, Shelby would marry Anton. Mother and Danny would leave for Lansing. Catherine would stay for one more evening and on Tuesday Romèe and she would start a tour of the continent.

Catherine had not dreamt of Joan of Arc for several days, not since Anton's rejection. Romèe seemed the focus of St. Joan's attention, which stood to reason. St. Joan needed Romèe and his father's influence to bring the Dome idea to fruition.

Catherine planned to visit Domremy to stand outside St. Joan's cottage with the village church a stone's throw to her right, as St. Joan had when she first heard voices of inspiration to save France.

Someone knocked twice.

"It's us, sleepy head," Romèe called. "Anton has a gift for you."

Catherine opened the door, a crack.

Romèe picked her up then put her down on the small room's bed. "Look what Anton's brought you."

Anton leaned the large, framed nude sketch against the pillows.

"It is beautiful," Catherine and Romèe said in unison then laughed in relief at what could have been an awkward situation.

Anton took Romèe's arm as if to pull him out of the small room. "You promised to supervise the church decorations."

"No problem," Romèe said, holding securely to Catherine's hand.

"And your father says he needs to talk to you." Anton pulled at his own hair in frustration. It was obvious Romèe would not immediately follow him. "I have to go now."

Before Anton could bolt, Catherine gestured toward the six-foot drawing. "I don't know how to thank you for this."

Anton nodded and left, obviously nervous on his big day.

Romèe studied the sketch. "I will be hard to leave this behind while we travel. Is it all right to store it in the Artichoke house?"

"It will keep my place on the Mont warm." Catherine embraced him.

Romèe gently stroked her chin "May I show your sketches of the St. Joan's Dome to my father before I introduce you? I don't want your pretty face to take away from the professional drawings."

Here was what Catherine wanted, a man who valued her work. She quickly handed him all the sketchbooks.

Romèe kissed her mouth, one hand on her shoulder.

Catherine wanted him to stay and took a step closer. "You're pretty easy to love."

Romèe kissed her again soundly. "This will have to do until after lunch. I'm directing the decorating crew. Would you like a hike up to the Abbey when I'm done? We'll have plenty of time to dress for dinner."

"Please collect me."

After he left, Catherine moved toward the bathroom for a shower. However, Mother's familiar knock on her door interrupted her plan.

"Are you pregnant?" Mother demanded.

"I'm a virgin on the pill."

Mother collapsed on the bed. "I dreamt St. Joan's Dome was your stomach."

"I wondered why I hadn't dreamt of St. Joan lately."

"You're the most important thing in my life. Your children will be that important to you, too."

"More important than husbands?"

"I guarantee it. Partners are all very well, but children are immortality."

Mother noticed the nude portrait. "Your hair. We have to pick up your wig. This is beautiful work. I'd like Danny to see it."

"No problem," Catherine said. "Romèe's going to store the picture for me in the Artichoke house. He's showing my drawings to his father before he meets me."

"Danny already knows your worth," Mother said. "Let's show him what started all the trouble."

"Give me half-an-hour to dress," Catherine begged, "then you can bring him by. I need to eat."

"I'll wait for you," Mother said. "Tell me all about last night."

Once Catherine was dressed, Mother took one end of the framed drawing. After her mother looked up and down the hall to see if the coast was clear, Catherine helped her carry the sketch next door to Danny and Mother's room.

"I've just ordered coffee from room service," Danny said in greeting, before turning to Catherine. "You worried your mother last night." Mother and Catherine turned the frame around so he could see the sketch. "And what's this?"

"Catherine with hair," Mother crowed.

They stood in silence, admiring the art.

Danny finally said, "You are a beautiful woman, Catherine. Now let me see those sketches of St. Joan's Dome."

"Romèe took them," Catherine said.

"Took them!" Danny's Italian nature made him bluster about. Danny stopped behind a stuffed chair and his hands beat a tattoo on the upholstery. "That rich kid has a thing or two to learn."

Mother laughed at him, "Isn't he magnificent?"

"This must be what Zeus looked like, storming around heaven." Catherine imitated Danny's protruding jaw, fist beating the opposite palm. "Steal fire? I'll let a hawk eat his heart out."

Mother said. "Romèe's showing the sketches to his father."

"You could have told me," Danny said. "Zeus, huh. I like that."

"Let me get my albums. Romèe said we could leave them in his house too."

"House?" Danny asked.

Catherine let her mother explain as she raced to get the photographs. She propped the door open with a tennis shoe, then filled her arms with five albums, all of Mont Saint Michel.

She stopped for a moment before kicking the shoe away to close the door. The afternoon before Anton's fish soup, she had spent hours arranging the pictures. The same anticipation she felt then, she felt now. This was better. Now her life spread out into the future, then she had only thought of one night.

Back in Mother's room, Danny took the stack of books to the small couch. Mother joined him. The first album held a series of shots with Saint Michael's statue as the focal point of at least fifty carefully constructed photos.

"A pictographic record of a flight from reality," Mother said.

"Or escape from the disasters of the twentieth century," Danny echoed.

Catherine laughed. "Try the next one. An essay of stone, it follows the use of rock upon rock from the lichen covered inner walls to the pink and gray marble towers over the Grand Staircase.

Mother said. "You could name every stone in this pile."

"Someday, I'll introduce you. The pictures show the variety of construction in each century. But, I cannot figure out how the Almonry walls weathered inside. You can see the mortar outlasted the rock."

"Did they scrub the fireplace soot off?" Mother asked.

Danny said, "Maybe compression from the weight of the stories above."

Catherine persisted, "Some scientist knows, maybe a geologist. Mother, don't you think it's strange I don't dream of St. Joan anymore?"

"Stranger," Mother said, "is the fact from the reality of history, we know Joan of Arc. She was the first Existentialist, believing what she knew, not what she was taught."

"Is anyone too confident in the Lord?" Danny asked.

Catherine closed her albums. "The Mont epitomizes spiritual supremacy in life, while the ramparts symbolize the baser powers."

When Romèe came by after lunch, Catherine's first question was about her drawings.

"I didn't see my father when I dropped off the sketch pads." Romèe reached for Catherine's hand as they headed for the Abbey.

Was she wrong about him? Could she take off with this guy across the continent, maybe lose him in a crowd, get lost without knowing the language? What could happen? Surviving the night she had cut off her hair bestowed Catherine's confidence. "Where was your father? When will he see the sketches?"

"Plenty of time. I'll make sure he reviews each one of them, before I introduce you."

Patience was not one of Catherine's virtues. "I forgot to look up at the bells at the Angeles. The bells tolled for me."

"Hemmingway," Romèe gave her arm an understanding squeeze. "I'm sleeping in his room at my aunt's hotel. While you're getting your degree, I'll arrange the money for your commission."

"A competitive award?" Catherine worried.

"Not if I put up the money."

Catherine clapped her hands then she sobered, worrying how the Dome of St. Joan would fare if their relationship failed to develop.

"I promise," he said reading her mind. "No matter what happens between us."

Catherine swung her arms around his neck, "I am blessed to know you."

Romèe laughed. "Or, we're both possessed by St. Joan."

In her mother's suite Catherine and Mother admired Danny's ability to strut in his wedding tuxedo.

"Delia's a genius wig-maker," Mother said as the phone rang.

It was Shelby Constance inviting Mother and Catherine to help her get ready for the wedding rehearsal.

Mrs. Bermont and Shelby had waited for them in the Queen-of-Hearts room. Shelby's wedding dress hung on the outside of the closet door. Mrs. Bermont's wore a light blue suit, while Shelby was wearing a long shimmering gold cloth slip...not unlike the short tunic St. Joan wore in Catherine's dream.

"You're radiant." Mother touched Shelby's fingertips as if addressing a queen.

Catherine was amazed at the transformation of this gnome-like creature into a stately goddess. Heels and the upswept hairdo helped. "Mrs. Bermont," she said smiling at Shelby, "I wanted to compliment you on the filigree beadwork creation you made for Shelby's wedding. The dress is elegant."

Shelby voice shook from nerves. "Your hair is beautifully arranged." Addressing her future mother-in-law and Mother, she asked, "May I speak with Catherine alone?"

Catherine blushed, anticipating obvious questions about the nude sketch. "I wish you could have seen Anton's happiness when he discovered the dress."

Shelby waited to speak until both of the older women left. "Anton told me how much Romèe loves you." In an embarrassed burst of words she added, "Now that we're practically sister-in-laws, would you and your mother mind sitting on my side of the aisle in the cathedral. The nuns from the convent will be there; but with all of the friends Anton has invited, I'm afraid my showing of friends and family will be pitiful in comparison."

"We will be honored." Catherine hugged her new sister. "But the solution is to seat the guests randomly."

Shelby smiled in relief. She called in Mrs. Bermont and Mother who agreed Catherine's idea was the best answer.

***

As the wedding guests filed up the path leading to the Cathedral, Catherine noticed the coral sky matched her own dress.

Romèe met Mother, Danny and Catherine at the church door and ushered them to their seat. "This day was made for you," he whispered to Catherine. "The sky salutes every hair on your head."

Catherine smiled at his awareness of the coincidence of color. She did not enjoy wearing the wig, but held her head erect knowing its flower-bedecked, braided crown was stunning.

Mother and Danny walked behind them and Catherine caught her mother patting Romèe's back.

Even though they had arrived at the Choir a half-hour early, there was already a crush of people. Anton's friends from around the world gathered for the celebration.

White roses and lilies from the Laurent's Paris shop filled the altar. Garlands draped the pillars. The second tier of the Romanesque naves was festooned with hanging ivy and an explosion of colorful yellow, pink, and red flowers.

Shelby seemed to float down the petal-strewn aisle.

Father Damion officiated at the high mass, which included an incense-laden benediction. The combined odors were a powerful.

A gifted soprano sang, "Come Holy Ghost, Creator blessed, and in our hearts take up the rest. Come with Thy Grace and Heavenly aid to fill the hearts which Thou hast made, to fill the hearts which Thou hast made."

After the ceremony, Romèe breathed deeply as they waited for the wedding party outside the church on the west platform. "That was too much!" Catherine glanced at him with surprised disapproval. "The flowers and incense were overwhelming."

"It's worth the beauty," Mother said.

Catherine remembered, "The walls of the church used to be bright with paint."

"Could the painted walls be restored?" Danny asked.

No one seemed to know. They were interrupted by the flower girls, who handed them packages of white lily petals to toss at the bride and groom.

Mother and Catherine winked at each other. They knew the flower petals were St. Joan's doing. As Shelby and Anton came out of the church, the wedding party showered them with the lilies.

The coral-colored reception tents on the west platform terrace flapped with a mild June breeze. The orchestra would play until midnight. Romèe insisted Catherine sit with his mother and father. Jack Laurent was not quite as tall as his son, but seemed to tower over everyone. His stance was not bold or imposing, but he had a slow way of carrying himself which demanded deference.

She listened carefully, as Romèe explained his own plans for opening a flower shop on the Mont. Jack and Bernice Laurent did not comment, as if their son's plans were of no consequence.

Instead, Jack directed his inquiries to Catherine. "And what are your plans for our son, Miss Marksteiner?"

"Catherine," she allowed automatically. "I'd like to get to know Romèe better."

"How will that help you build your Dome?" Mr. Laurent asked.

Questioning her motives, was he? Romèe was oblivious to the challenge. He contentedly devoured an entire barbecued chicken. Surprised at her own conviction, Catherine said, "If St. Joan wants her Dome, she'll get it."

Mr. Laurent said, "That's all well and good."

Was he encouraging her to argue? His demeanor gave no clue. He appeared innocently curious. Trying to draw Romèe's attention, Catherine said, "Romèe thinks I should show my sketches to schools on the continent. If they're interested, I would like to study in Europe."

Romèe heard. "Tell them how long you've loved the Mont."

"I first saw Mont Saint Michel's outline in the travel section of our newspaper in Ann Arbor. It reminded me of Walt Disney's castle logo. One-hundred and nineteen knights defended the Mont from England while Joan of Arc saved the rest of France. I've read everything I could find remotely connected to Mont Saint Michel or St. Joan. So, Mother and I planned for this week together; while Mother pursued the ghost of St. Joan."

"But the Maid found you." Mr. Laurent smiled. "And now my son has fallen in love with you."

"And I'm falling in love with him"

Romèe put his arm around her shoulders. "Joan of Arc crusaded for the souls of her countrymen before leading them to victory against the English. France would have no history if St. Joan hadn't envisioned a sovereign nation."

Catherine wrinkled her nose in disapproval before continuing. "Men talk about Napoleon until my teeth ache. That self-proclaimed Emperor annihilated the most perfect men out of three generations of Frenchmen.

Those fit for battle were cannon fodder for Bonaparte's egotistic attempts at conquest. France lost the First and Second World Wars because the courageous and gallant Frenchmen had been stomped into the ground by mad Napoleon."

Moving uncomfortably in his chair, as if to defend French manhood, Mr. Laurent resisted any attempt at a rebuttal, when Bernice, his wife, patted his hand.

Catherine continued, "Poor St. Joan was relegated to the tribe of mystics instead of her rightful place in history books. France needs to show its gratitude to their original savior."

Romèe's father continued the interrogation. "Who will finance the building project?"

"I don't have a clue. But remember St. Joan saw her Saints with 'her bodily eyes.' I think she wants a tangible symbol of inspiration for Frenchmen to enjoy."

Catherine she, was distracted by half listening to Romèe and her own mother discuss their upcoming trip.

When Romèe mentioned Rouen, Mother reminded him, "That's where they burned St. Joan at the stake." Mother could only remember one photograph of Rouen. "It shows Nazi soldiers at a shrine or fountain named after the saint."

Romèe knew the photo. "I've never been able to place where it was taken."

"Maybe it was destroyed in the bombings," Mrs. Laurent said.

"There are many sculptures of St. Joan in Rouen," Romèe said. "One is in a church on the spot where St. Joan was tied to the stake. And, in a modern complex near the middle of the town there is a giant statue of her, five men high."

"Are you planning to take my daughter to visit Florence?"

They discussed why Florence was a more pleasant city to visit, for free thinkers searching for art treasures, even more than Rome. Then Romèe said, "When St. Joan's Dome is completed, the tourist trade to the Mont will triple." Jack Laurent cocked his head to hear more. "Mont Saint Michel will be more famous to French Catholics than the Vatican. The twin patrons of France, Saint Michael and Joan of Arc, will combine their forces to protect and guide the Nation."

Mrs. Laurent asked Catherine, "Are you a Catholic?"

Catherine admitted she was not, really. "I believe in a spiritual world, but find the dictates of the Pope irrelevant."

Mr. Laurent congratulated her for being a devoted pupil of St. Joan. "The saint knew enough to question authority - even when it cost her life."

"But not her soul!" Catherine said.

"We're leaving our son in good hands," Mrs. Laurent said.

Anton and Shelby came up to their table. Shelby leaned over Catherine's mother, "You might have to lose your daughter to the Mont but Anton tells me she will construct a jewel for the world to honor Joan of Arc."

Then Danny reached up and touched her mother's face with the palm of his hand. Catherine knew by his expression he cherished her mother. Mother made her way around the table to Catherine. Catherine stood up to speak with her.

Mother took Catherine's face in her hands, kissing her forehead and cheeks as punctuation marks at the end of each sentence. "This holiday has contained all the travail of a birthing trauma. Now it's crowned with Romèe's assured affection."

Catherine clasped her mother's hands to her heart. "Happiness lurks behind every corner, and still my heart is breaking."

Mother hugged her and whispered. "Hearts know no distance. Mine beats with yours." Mother joined Danny. Catherine extended an arm in their direction as they descended the Abbey's steps, off for their trip to America. Mother waved and turned away.

Romèe came to Catherine's side. She could not seem to lower her arm, raised in farewell. Finally, Romèe grasped Catherine's arm, entwined it with his own.

EPILOGUE

2033

Twenty years after Anton's wedding, Romèe called out onto the terraced garden. "Cousins, cousins." Fifteen teenage children broke up their soccer game to help him distribute a tray of iced tea.

From the roof-patio, Catherine put finishing touches on a watercolor of Joan of Arc's Dome. She was torn between the two views, the beauty of the rose crystal addition to the cathedral and her children in the garden.

Anton and Shelby's seven and her own eight made a great clan. There were three redheads, two girls and a boy of hers, and four blond boys of Anton's. The rest were as dark as Italians.

As Catherine turned toward the Dome of St. Joan, a wave of affection flowed through her.

Joan of Arc's spirit was thanking her again.

Catherine chose her smallest brush to dab blue dots in ceilings on her easel to hint at the blue butterflies fluttering among the flowering trellises in the dome. The many faceted Dome balanced the peaks of the Melville into a perfect marriage of technological excellence and ancient romance.

Mont Saint Michel had become the most frequented tourist site in Europe. Tickets were issued for a tour beginning in Avranches at noon. The islanders had the mornings and evenings free to pursue normal lives for their families.

Mother, widowed at seventy-five, and a bit frail, threw her handkerchief into Catherine's paint box to get her attention. "Where's the young girl who realized her dreams?"

"I'm fifty now."

"I meant Joan of Arc." Mother grinned.

"That war waif, who took on whole armies and church elders to help her country? She's happy with her tribute, I guess."

"I suppose I'll have great grandchildren to look forward to in five more years?"

Catherine poured her mother another glass of iced tea. "If not sooner. The troops will all be up for lunch in a minute. Do you want to go in before they get here?"

"Absolutely, not. How can I hassle them, if I'm quietly lying down?"

"They'd complain too, if you weren't here to listen to their latest exploits." They watched the group of noisy teenagers advance.

The End

Printed in the United States
By Bookmasters